Chapter One

CW00496992

Saturday

The Reverend Timothy Marsh stood in the doorway of St Augustine's church, looking out across the graveyard. In front of him were headstones of marble and granite monuments to lost loved ones. The black cassock he wore stood out, a sharp contrast against his snow-white hair. Around his waist was a wide, black tasselled sash, and a large gold cross hung from his neck. Many of his congregation, he knew, said that life and old age had caught up with him. Sometimes his sermons like him seemed vague and hard to understand. At seventy-eight, he still tried to look manly and present an agile figure to his parishioners, but beneath the black robe lay a tired older man.

It wasn't until after the christening at midday that Tom Craddock, the sexton, discovered a body in the far corner of the graveyard. He spotted a man under the shade of the Yew tree. He was sitting with his back against a headstone. Spying the bottle alongside him and the vomit on the front of his shirt, the sexton immediately thought the man was a drunk, sleeping it off. Craddock dismounted from his ride-on mower and tried to rouse the man but got no response. Realizing he was dead, the horrified sexton immediately leapt onto his mower and zig-zagged his way through the gravestones, calling loudly for Reverent Marsh.

Because of the bodies and proximity to the low wall that separated Miller's Lane from the graveyard, the police had erected a canvas screen. Reid had asked for it to be put in place after Reverent Marsh said villagers would gather on the sports ground that afternoon. There was to be a children's football match, and they'd have to pass the graveyard to get there. It was not a sight that children should see, Marsh told Reid. Because no crime scene officers had been called, a canvas scene had to be brought across the road from the scout hut. Using poles from one of the scout's tents, it had only taken Reid, Cotton, and the other two constables a few minutes to erect it.

Reverent Marsh came out of the porch into the sunlight and sat on the wooden seat beside the door. Taking out his glasses, he polished them with his handkerchief. He put them on and looked at the grass between the headstones that the sexton had been mowing. The police had stopped that, but it still needed to be finished. Also, the altar brasses had to be polished, and flowers put out. Tomorrow was Sunday. It was going to be a busy day. Not counting the usual morning service, there was to be another christening straight after a wedding. Then, on Monday, the funeral of old Mr Grimes, the village chemist. He thought about getting Mrs Craddock, the sexton's wife, to do the brasses first thing in the morning. He wanted it all to look nice.

The old vicar directed his gaze to the goings on over on the far side of the cemetery and then turned his attention back to the path leading to the road. At the bottom, under the porch of the lynch gate, two uniformed constables stood talking. Opposite, on the grass verge, stood two patrol cars and an ambulance. The ambulance had been there with its back doors open and the crew sitting on the back step enjoying the spring sunshine for the last hour. Now it was moving off. The big black van from the mortuary took its spot.

Reverent Marsh wondered how long the police would be here. It worried him. Was there any likelihood of keeping the church closed tomorrow? If it was, he'd need time to move everything to Saint Mary's. The christening and the wedding will be ok, but the funeral was another matter. No cremation for him. The site for old Grimes's internment had all already been prepared. They'll have to keep him on ice a little longer if it needs to be postponed. I'll have to ask the officer in charge, he thought. He seems a nice man! A reasonable one, too, he hoped. What was his name again? He ran his hands through his thinning hair. His mind was not as sharp as it used to be. Then it came to him. Ah, yes! Reid! Detective Inspector Reid!

****

Mike Reid came out from behind the blue tarpaulin screen, moved away from the shade of the tree, and stood looking around, the late afternoon sun warm on his shoulders. The long, cold winter had passed. Hibernating creatures awakened as the countryside came alive. The earth came to life again, and as the soils slowly warmed, farmers and gardeners started planting seeds. Bluebells now carpeted the woodlands. Spring now had a solid foothold, and there was no going back. Beside the pathway, between the headstones, purple, yellow, and orange crocuses and a few stray daffodils blossomed. In the cherry orchards, which Reid had passed on the way to the church, buds were bursting into flowers. A new season, a new beginning.

Reid turned to PC Cotton. 'You can call the van and have them take him away. We're done here.' Reid sighed as he checked his phone, ensuring he had all the photos he wanted. 'I don't know why CID got called in?' PC Cotton stood in silence, hands behind his back, looking at Reid. It was a look that said *it wasn't me. I didn't call it in.* Cotton nodded, then walked off, talking into his shoulder mic. The attending physician, an elderly local doctor, had been called in. He hadn't stayed long. He hastily examined the body and declared life extinct. He said he could not fully determine the cause of death and would inform the coroner. There'd have to be an autopsy. He bid Reid a good afternoon, then excused himself, saying he had other urgent matters to attend to.

After he'd gone, Reid looked across the graveyard at the yellow daffodils around the base of the yew trees as they bobbed and swayed in the afternoon breeze. As the afternoon progressed, the southerly had gotten stronger. Reid sniffed the air a few times, taking in the unmistakable smell of the sea.

Finally, he looked up at the church clock. It was four o'clock. He looked across the graveyard and then set off towards the church.

The church of St Augustine in the tiny hamlet of Corn Hill had looked down over the town for fourteen hundred years. It stood high on the cliff-top and had survived the Vikings, the Norman conquest, Henry the eighth, and three civil wars. In World War Two, Hitler's big guns on the French coast had taken a couple of potshots at it. One shell landed close. For once, it was welcomed because, during one Sunday service, it landed in the field opposite. The casualty was a cow, killed by flying shrapnel.

Sitting in the congregation that Sunday morning was the village butcher. By evening, and with meat on ration, the carcass had been removed. The following Sunday, they all gathered in the church and sang, "All creatures Great And Small." Then, after the sermon about which thou shall not covet thy neighbor's ox, all the village, including the vicar, gathered in the church hall for a roast beef and Yorkshire pudding lunch.

The church, built in 610 AD, was in memory of Augustine, the first Archbishop, who'd died six years earlier. In this church, knights, who had set forth to fight in the crusades in the Holy Land, came to pray before leaving England's shores.

In the fifteenth century, parishioners would hang a burning beacon from the church spire if they knew a ship was due at night. Sailors could see the beacon far out at sea, a guiding light to help mariners navigate their way down the channel, passed the Goodwin Sands into the sheltered waters of the harbour. Charles Dickens often visited this church. It was said the early morning, mist-enshrouded graveyard inspired him to write Bleak House.

Seeing Reid approaching, the vicar removed his glasses, placed them in his pocket, and rose from his seat. He stood, running his hands down the front of his cassock.

'Constable Cotton said you wanted to see me, vicar?' Reid said as he approached.

Reverent Marsh looked confused for a moment. 'Did I? Ah, yes. The constable at the gate. You needn't have come all this way over, Detective Inspector. I was about to come and see you.'

He watched the black van from the morgue make its way around the perimeter road to the other side of the graveyard. Turning back to face Reid, he said, 'I wanted to see you, Inspector, because I was concerned about tomorrow. I spoke to the constable at the gate. He said he couldn't help, and I was to see you. I have morning service, a christening at eleven-thirty, a wedding at one and a funeral to perform on Monday. If we're still closed to the public, I'll have to plan to have them moved over to Saint Michael's. That doesn't leave me much time. People need to be informed, and the burial service will have to be postponed. The undertakers and the family will need to be informed.'

Reid gave the vicar a reassuring smile. 'It's okay, reverend. All can go ahead. We'll be taking the body away shortly.'

'That's a load off my mind.' The old vicar cast an eye on the activity on the other side of the graveyard.

Following the vicar's gaze, Reid turned. 'As you can see, the van is on its way over there as we speak. I shall return to Kingsport, and in an hour, you should have your churchyard all back to normal.'

'It was a tragedy what happened. I said a prayer for that poor man. But it's a relief to know that I can carry on. Tell me. Was it the drink that took him? I only asked because when the sexton called me and came to look, I couldn't help but notice the whiskey bottle and all the vomit.'

'Well, I'm afraid I can't say for sure, but the doctor thinks he choked on his vomit. We'll have to wait for the postmortem results to tell us that. Your sexton! I spoke to him. He told me you'd seen that man around here before. Is that right?'

'Aye, yes, Inspector. I did that. It was about a week ago. I saw him when I came from the presbytery to pick up some things from the vestiary. I remember it clearly because it rained that morning. Coming in through the gate on the east side, I looked over and saw him sheltering in the lynch gate. He'd gone when I went out a quarter of an hour later. That was the first time I saw him. Who was he, Inspector? Do you know? He didn't look like the homeless type because he was well dressed.'

'No. I'm afraid we don't know yet who the man is. There was no identification on him. You say you saw him again then?' asked Reid. 'When was that?'

'Yes, at least twice since. I saw that man walking among the gravestones. I asked him if he was looking for anyone in particular, and he said he was researching something and found what he was after.'

'Did he say what it was?'

'No, Inspector, he didn't. One thing I will say, he did smell of the drink.'

'When was the last time you saw him?'

'That would be yesterday, Friday. Just after seven in the morning.' He answered. 'He never saw me because he was sitting in a back pew. I think he was using one of those small electronic gadgets. It was small. A tablet, I think you call them?' The old vicar laughed. ' I bet Moses would have loved one of those? Instead of having to chisel out the ten commandments, he could have just typed them out in minutes!' He laughed at his joke, then said, 'I had the feeling he may have slept there overnight. The second time I saw him was two days ago. He was standing near the stone wall, where he lay now.'

'I take it you don't lock the church at night?'

'No. It's a sanctuary for anyone in need of spiritual guidance. Day or night.' the vicar answered, looking towards the heavens.

Reid turned and looked towards the church door.

Sitting back on the seat, Marsh said, 'He could have been around longer.'

'So, he never introduced himself or said where he came from or what he was looking for?' Reid asked, sitting down beside him.

Taking out a hanky, Reverent Marsh took out his glasses and slowly set about polishing the lenses. Putting them on, he said, 'No, Inspector. I'm afraid not. I asked him. He never said what he was looking for, only that he'd found what he wanted. I assumed he was looking for a grave. A relative, maybe? Researching his family tree, maybe? Many people nowadays want to know their family history and where they came from.' He turned to Reid and asked, 'Was there nothing to identify him?'

'No, I'm afraid not; there was nothing at all. Not even a wallet.'

'How strange!' replied the vicar. 'The day I spoke to him, he was on a mobile phone talking to someone. He also had a small red backpack like school children use.'

Reid thought earlier when he searched the body that maybe someone had come across him lying there and, thinking he was in a drunken stupor, stole his wallet. Reid's thoughts went to the tablet and phone. New information! Could he have been drinking with someone else? It seemed whoever took the wallet may have taken them as well.

'The backpack! Did he have it with him when you saw him yesterday?' enquired Reid.

'I can't be sure because he was at the other end of the church and the light was poor. I came in through the vestry door to pick up the Sunday sermon I'd left there the day before, and I only stayed for a few minutes, then went.'

Reid got to his feet, walked over to the church door, pushed it open, and went in. He stood for a few moments in the doorway, letting his eyes adjust to the dim surroundings. He moved a few paces, then stopped. The sunlight streaming through the stained-glass windows set a pattern of mosaic colours dancing across the floor. Reid slowly walked down the aisle, searching between and beneath the pews.

The worn flagstone beneath his feet bore testament to the many worshippers that had gone before him. As he moved from row to row, he wondered whether this quiet air, smelling of candles and the churchy smell of musty prayer books, metal polish and flowers, had sensed the same to the dead man. Reverent Marsh stood by the door, curiously watching his every move. After finding nothing, Reid came out from the pew and headed back up the aisle to the door. His heels clicking on the flagstones sounded loud in the confines of the small church.

As he came out into the sunlight, a constable came up the path towards him, the gravel crunching under his shoes. 'We're all done, sir. The vicar can have his churchyard back. Everything's packed away. Is there anything else you want us for?'

Reid turned, his eyes staring out across the graveyard. 'Yes, but first, take the tarp back to the scout hut, will you?' Then, turning to the vicar, Reid said, 'By the way, thank you for letting us use it.'

Reid moved away, taking the constable with him.

'When you've done that, I want you all to search this entire area for a red backpack, a mobile phone and a tablet. The deceased was seen to have had those with him. '

'I'll come and unlock the hut for you, constable,' called Marsh. From the pocket of his cassock, he pulled out a bunch of keys. Continuing, he said, 'Then I must go in search of the sexton. This grass won't cut itself and needs to be finished.'

After the constable and Reverent Marsh had left, Reid looked across the graveyard. The two attendants were now placing the body bag in the van. Here we have a reasonably well-dressed man, maybe sleeping rough and without identification. No wallet, no phone, nothing. What was it that brought him here in this churchyard in the first place? Who is this nameless man? Someone must miss him. Reid had already checked with Luke Hollingsworth, and nobody answering the man's description had been reported missing. His phone interrupted further thought, vibrating against his thigh. He took it from his pocket and read the message. It was from Emma.

Don't forget. Pick up your stripes from dry cleaners. It would help if you looked nice at the party. Don't be late.
Luv yer, Em

Oh hell. The suite! Reid thought. The one with the stripes. I wouldn't say I like that one. He thought it made him look like one of those cheap, cigar-sucking lawyers he'd see on American TV shows. Emma wanted him to look his best for Baxter's going away party.

Reid thumbed in a reply. I am leaving soon. Back well in time—Luv yer 2.

He hit send.

Chapter Two

Sunday

The glass of the mullioned window cast a chequerboard pattern of morning sunlight across the polished walnut floor. The curtain moved gently in the breeze. In the distance, a church bell summoned the faithful to morning prayer. The words from the Monkey's song, 'A Pleasant Valley Sunday,' came into Carter's head as he lay there, staring up at the black oak beams of the ceiling. Christine lay sleeping beside him. Her breathing was gentle and even.

Carter turned his head slowly to the left. Not too bad! He turned it to the right. Still good. At least his head was still attached to his shoulders. All things considered, he felt good after last night. Not even a headache. Ted Baxter's farewell bash and Mike Reid's promotion had gone off well, with drink flowing freely all evening. Ted Baxter was leaving in three days to take on his new role as a training officer at the Brisbane Police Training College in Australia. He and Ted had been together for a long time. They made a good pair, and Carter would miss him. Even Commander Janice Watkins had popped in, wished him luck, and stayed for a few.

Baxter's send-off had gone well. Too well! Carter lay trying to remember how many he'd put away. Mixing beer with whisky was never a good thing. It was a sure recipe for disaster. The celebration continued until well after the Black Bull closed, everyone dancing like they'd forgotten how to stand still. Carter admitted to having two left feet and not being much of a dancer. He lost count of how many times he had squished Christine's foot under his. Still, she smiled brightly as their heels clicked over the floor. He remembered Luke Hollingsworth being under the weather, moving around the floor like a limbo dancer in a spaghetti factory. In the end, George Sutton, the landlord of the Black Bear, had to push everyone out of the door.

Carter threw back the covers and placed his feet on the cold, bare boards. He got up, went to the window, pushed back the curtain, and looked out. It was a view he never tired of. To him, the countryside was a beautiful swathe of rolling green divided by walls of mossy grey stone, picturesque by any standards. For many, it was just grass, grass, and more grass. Carter wondered how many noticed the wide variety of trees, birds, and animals that called the countryside their home. Across the lane from the cottage was a large meadow. In it, a movement caught his eye. Peeking out from the tall grass, he saw a fox's head. It turned its head, looked at him, and in a flash, it was gone. Spring was lambing season, and there was no food shortage for a Vixen looking to feed her ever-growing family of pups.

Not wanting to wake Christine, he quietly dressed, pulling on a pair of tracksuit bottoms. Picking up the T-shirt from the back of the chair he'd worn the night before, he inspected it, sniffed it, and then tossed it into the washing basket. Then, grabbing a clean one from the chest of drawers, he slipped it over his head. He then padded off along the landing to the toilet. After spending a few minutes there, he headed down the stairs and into the kitchen.

After Carter turned on the TV, he popped two eggs into a saucepan and put them on the stove to boil. Moving to the other side of the kitchen, he dropped two slices of bread into the toaster. He then set out the tea tray with a small vase and placed a single red rose in it. After making a pot the tea, and seeing all was ready, Carter put the card and a little box on the tray and carried it to the bedroom. Pushing open the door with his foot, he walked in.

'Wakey, wakey sleepy head. It's a beautiful morning, and I've brought you breakfast.'

Christine sat up in bed, rubbed the remains of sleep from her eyes, and then gazed at him, a warm smile spreading over her face.

Placing the tray on the bed, he bent over and kissed her. 'Happy anniversary.' She kissed him back.

After reading the card, she reached out and opened the box. Inside, attached to a gold chain, was a heart-shaped pennant made of china set in a gold frame. Engraved on it were their initials and the date of marriage.

'It's beautiful,' she said, holding it up. 'And you remembered that china is the gift to be given for a second anniversary?'

A guilty look spread across his face. 'Er, no. I admit I had a bit of help on that one. Err, Google and Marcia.'

She laughed. 'It's lovely.' She pulled him forward and kissed him.

'Eat up before your eggs get cold.'

They sat talking about the first time they'd met and the circumstances surrounding it. After Christine finished, Carter took the tray and placed it on the bedside table.

'To celebrate, I've booked us a table at that little pub in Canterbury for Sunday lunch. You know, the one. The one by the river? The Three Swans. After, if you like, we can take a punt on the river or stroll around the cathedral?'

Carter enjoyed strolling through Canterbury's old narrow backstreets, trolling through its book shops and enjoying its century-old architecture. Starting as a young PC on the beat at eighteen back in 1990, he'd policed those streets in all weathers, getting to know every local and shopkeeper. Thirty years on, and here he was, a DCI.

She beckoned with her finger. 'Come here. You need a reward for all that hard work that went into making my breakfast.' Then, smiling, she threw back the bedsheet. 'Get in. I'm in control this time, so you be a good boy and don't move your hands. I'm going to drive you crazy, then stop, then do it all over again until you beg me to finish this. Even then, I won't. I'm just gonna do every naughty thing to you until you arrest me and put me in handcuffs.'

Outside, birds were singing. Inside, so was Carter. This, he thought, was definitely going to be a pleasant valley Sunday.

Chapter Three

From his top-floor flat overlooking the harbour, Dave Penrose pulled aside the curtains covering the glass sliding doors. Pushing them apart, he took a few tentative steps out onto the balcony, breathed in the morning air, and stretched. Then, turning, he slowly scanned the length of the Marine Parade. Finally, his eyes came to rest on the clock tower at the far end by the Wellington Docks. Its hands were showing seven-thirty. The stiffening breeze whipping across the harbour's choppy waters brought with it the taste of the ocean. Penrose's father died six years earlier, leaving him a sizable amount of money in his will. The comfortable two-bedroom flat had a sitting room, a bathroom with a cubicle shower, and a good-sized kitchen area. It was a brilliant investment.

Living directly across the hall from him was a group of Chinese students. On the whole, they were quiet, and he hardly heard them. Penrose wasn't sure how many shared it, but there were at least three, maybe four. He understood from the other two tenants on his floor that the students were studying at Canterbury University. Penrose knew one who worked part-time in a restaurant on Castle Street. He only knew this because he had once stopped off for a takeaway on his way home one night.

Stifling a yawn, he turned and looked towards the cliffs. They rose from the sea, towering chalk ramparts coloured crimson by the rising sun. This is the best part of the day, the early morning. Clean, new and refreshing. Yachts in the harbour rose and fell, tugging on their mooring as they rode the incoming tide. He could see container and cargo ships moving up and down the channel. The 'Pride Of Kent', one of the many channel ferries that crossed between Dover and France, was clearing the breakwater.

A not-so-uncommon sight, one Penrose often saw, was a Border Force patrol vessel coming through the western entrance of the harbour. Refugees could often be seen on deck after being rescued while trying to attempt the crossing to England. He knew four had drowned attempting the perilous channel crossing last week using an inflatable in rough weather.

Shifting his gaze, he spots the man walking a dog along the promenade, a regular walker. Another who, like himself, likes the mornings. The man posed as a lonely figure. A silly thought, but Penrose wondered if he was married. Somehow, he doubted it. The man entered the shelter, sat down on the bench, and pulled a newspaper from his jacket pocket. Penrose knew he'd be sitting there for fifteen minutes before moving on. It was a ritual.

Hearing a sound, he saw Marcia Kirby standing in the bathroom doorway. She had just come from the shower, a towel wrapped around her head. Kirby stood there, doing the buttons up on her blouse. She was hungover, tired, and had a grumbling stomach and a headache.

'Some say the only way to avoid a hangover is not to drink too much in the first place!' Penrose said.

'It's sympathy I want, not a bleeding lecture from you, smart arse. Anyway, you didn't do too bad, either. I won't be the only one with a thick head this morning, and if I remember rightly, there'll be a few others.' She came and sat down at the table and poured herself a glass of orange juice from the jug Penrose had put out for breakfast.

'What do you fancy for breakfast? How about a fry-up? The full works. There's nothing better than a full English breakfast to curer a hangover.'

She looked at him, a distasteful look creeping across her face. 'Yuck! Dave Penrose, you're a bleeding masochist. Coffee and aspirins on toast will do me just fine.'

She rubbed her hair with the towel, and as Penrose disappeared into the kitchen; she called after him. 'Have you thought any more about the DCI's offer last night?'

Penrose came back and stood in the doorway. 'About me joining the team at Kent Street? How much of that was drink, and how much of it was sincerity?'

She stood up. 'That's not fair, Dave, and you know it. As you know, Bob Carter is a good boss to work for, and he thinks a lot of you! He knows you're good at what you do and reliable. You're committed to the job. He knows that, so he wants you on his team.'

'You seem to have forgotten about our talk and us working together. We both said we should keep the job and our private life separate! How do you think that would work out?'

'I know of at least four couples working together in our division. And two, married.'

'You seem to forget, Marcia. We decided some time back to keep our work and relationship separate. Besides, I'm up for a promotion soon.'

She sat back down. 'What?' She stared across the room at him.

'Yer. DI Marchbanks, Jerry, he's going. His time is up. He's recommending me for the position. Marchbanks reckons there's no problem in me getting it. Jerry told me he's had words with those on high. The job is mine if I want it. He said I'm a dead cert, and if I moved to Kingsport, I'd miss out on that, wouldn't I?'

'You never told me about that!'

'He only told me two days ago. Nothing's official yet, so keep it under your hat. Anyway,' he smiled, pointing to the open door of the balcony. 'Look at that view. Would you give that up?' Penrose turned and walked back into the kitchen.

'Inspector Penrose. It has a certain ring about it.' she said. 'When will you know for sure?'

'Maybe in a couple of days!' he replied.

After a few minutes, Kirby got up from the table and went to the kitchen. The smell of the frying bacon filled her nostrils, making her feel nauseous. Leaning against the door frame, she watched him crack two eggs into the frying pan.

'Sure, you won't have a fry-up? I'm doing fried bread!' he asked.

Her stomach lurched. She heaved, put her hand to her mouth, and raced to the bathroom.

Penrose smiled, grabbed two more rashers of bacon, and laid them in the frying pan.

'I love the smell of bacon frying in the morning.'

There came the distant sound of reaching them a few moments later, the sound of the toilet being flushed., Kirby emerged, herself looking a little flushed herself.

'Feeling better?' he asked as she walked back into the kitchen.

She nodded.

Chapter Four

Monday

When Carter walked in through the reception area that morning, Tom Crane, the custody sergeant, looked up from the newspaper he was reading on the counter. 'Morning, sir. You 'ave a good weekend?'

Carter smiled as he remembered the Sunday morning in the bedroom. Not bad going for an old guy? 'Aye, Tom, I did, thanks.'

'Great send-off for the DI, the other night, wasn't it, sir? I bet there were a few sore heads the next morning. I know mine was.' He then said. 'You're in early?'

'Paperwork. I've been putting it off for weeks, and I can't put it off any longer. If I don't have it in by the end of the week, the commander will have me castrated.'

Crane pulled a face.

As Carter spook, PC Mike Cotton came along the passage from the communications room into the custody area. Trailing behind him came PC Tony Best. Spotting Crane, Cotton said, 'Sarge. Another of those blooming sinkholes has opened up.'

'Fourth one this year, if I'm not mistaken?' said Crane, sourcing his mental records.

Slipping his arms into his Hi-Vis jacket, Best said, 'A big one, by the sounds of it, has opened up over at Snowdon. It's on the west side of the railway line, just off Holt Street. It's in Oxney Wood, close to the old colliery. The farmer that reported it said there's something there that shouldn't be! Probably some blasted sheep or cow has fallen down the hole. We're off over there now.'

Crane said to them, 'And lads. A word of caution! Don't forget that today is April the first, so don't make fools of yourself. We've already had a report of an alien with a big dangly thing running naked around Tesco's car park.'

'Don't worry, sarge. They'll have to get up early to pull the wool over our eyes. 'He winked at his partner, Tony Best. As if seeing Carter for the first time, PC Cotton said, 'Oh, morning, sir. Sorry I didn't see you there!'

Carter nodded. 'Morning,' then moved to one side, allowing the pair to pass

Before heading up to the CID suite on the first floor, Carter pushed through the swing doors and walked down the passage to the newly installed vending machines outside the locker rooms. When the canteen was closed, this was where you could get chocolate bars, sandwiches, tea or coffee. He knew those working over the weekend would have used up most of the CID supplies of coffee, so all would be scarce on a Monday morning. Carter popped two one-pound coins in the slot, selected his choice of coffee, placed a paper cup under the dispenser, pressed the button, and waited…… and waited. No liquid came out. Frustrated, he was about to hit the machine when suddenly, it gurgled, hissed, spat out a few drops of brown watery stuff, and then fell silent. He waited a little longer for something to happen, then banged his fist on the side. Still, the machine refused to give up its contents.

The door to the locker room swung open, and PC Stanton came out and was about to walk off in the opposite direction when he noticed Carter staring into the empty cup.

'It's buggered, sir. It hasn't worked since Friday. A notice was stuck on it, but it must have fallen off. They're supposed to be coming to fix it today.'

'Shit.' Carter looked at his watch. Six-thirty. Reaching for his wallet, he took out a five-pound note and handed it to Stanton. 'Here. Be a good lad and hop down to the café on the corner for me, and get me one. Milk, two sugars!' He then turned and walked off. As he neared the stairs, he called, 'And bring me back the change.'

The new computer screen was the first thing Carter noticed as he walked into his office. The screen was much bigger than his old one. Also, there was now a big tv screen up on the wall. This doubled as a conference monitor linked to the police network. Five minutes later, there was a knock on the door. Without waiting to be summoned, PC Stanton marched straight in, Styrofoam cup in hand.

'Ah, good man. You found me one.'

Stanton placed it down on the desk. 'Milk, two sugars, sir.' He fished the change out of his trouser pocket, handed it over to Carter, turned, and left. As the retreating constable moved towards the open door, Carter said, 'Thank you, constable.' Carter picked up the coffee cup, took a few sips, leaned back in his chair, and switched on the TV. He watched the news on the BBC for a while and, finding nothing of interest, switched it off.

Carter had come in early that morning, ahead of the others, to catch up on paperwork. He'd been putting it off for over a week. After finishing his coffee, Carter tossed the empty cup into the wastepaper basket. Then he pulled open the top drawer of his desk, took out the file marked Financial Forward Budget Estimates, and sighed. Commander Watkins had, twice last week, asked about its progress. Each time, his answer was the same. 'It's nearly finished, he said.' The truth be known, he hadn't even started on the blasted thing. She told him it had to be in by the nineteenth. He knew he couldn't put it off any longer. Today was the day, the nineteenth. He shook his head, sighed and brought up Microsoft Word, turning on the computer. Staring at the screen, he pondered on it for a few moments, pulled the keyboard closer and set to work.

****

Carter was thinking about going for another coffee when a knock came on the door. He looked up to see DS Mike Reid standing in the doorway.

'Got a minute, boss?' Reid asked.

Carter beckoned him in. Looking up at the wall clock, Carter was surprised to see it had gone eleven. Four hours had slipped by.

'Mike! Hi.'

'Morning, boss!' He looked over at the wall. 'Ah. I see you've got all the new teleconference stuff installed?' Then, looking at the papers strewn over the desk, he asked. 'Are you working on the budget? I thought you told the commander on Saturday night you'd finished it?'

Carter, glad of the interruption, leant back in his chair, raised his arms above his head, and stretched.

'Yer. Little white lie. What she doesn't know won't hurt her. This is the last page.' He stared at the computer screen. 'Even with Commander Watkins signing off on it, it still has to go before the finance committee. I'll be happy if this department gets half of what I put in for. With these overtime restraints, budget cuts and a staff shortage, it's a bloody nightmare. If we get more funding cuts, we won't have a bleeding police force. The uniform branch is already asking Special Constables to work more hours. They don't get paid, so that should please those on high! And they still want me to cut my department spending by ten, bleedin' per cent.'

'I wouldn't want to be in your shoes if you don't get this in by today. The commander was not in a good mood when I ran into her downstairs ten minutes ago. She was bollocking Inspector McNeil, and it sounded like he'd not sent his in. She did not sound too pleased.'

'Maybe he didn't trim off his ten per cent?' He eyed Reid thoughtfully, then said, 'Any progress on that body found in the Corn Hill churchyard?'

Unbuttoning his jacket, Reid sat down. 'No. Not a blooming thing. So far, we've drawn a total blank with no labels on his clothes. Doc Broadbent's finished the autopsy.'

'Did they find anything, the cause of death?'

'They didn't say, only that I should come over today. You know what Doc Broadbent is like, full of dramatics! So, I just thought I'd let you know that's where I'm off to now! Oh! And I contacted the press office and asked them to send his picture to all the media outlets. I'm hoping to get something back from that. They should be able to get it on the mid-day news. The only potential lead we have is the whiskey bottle!' Reid leant forward in his chair. 'It's not your usual stuff! It's not gut rot. This one is expensive. It's Johnnie Walker's Blue Label. It's not to be sniffed at, either. We're talking about a hundred and fifty quid a bottle. There can't be many places in town that would stock that, and few people could afford to buy it. I wish I could. I've got Dave Lynch out scouring the town, finding out who stocks it.'

Carter swiveled his desk chair around until he sat facing the window. He could see out across the Kent Street Memorial Park, where the Kingsport Annual Spring Flower Festival was being held. People came from far and wide to visit, photograph, and admire the display. This time of the year, it was a mass of colour. There were impressive borders of colourful tulips, daffodils and Amaryllis, all planted in large groups of the same colour and variety. The display was enough to satisfy the most demanding garden lover. He thought about what Christine had said to him only yesterday, that now would be an excellent time to prune and clean up their rose beds.

He spun around, turning his attention back to Reid. 'What about Dave? Do you think he's up to the job?'

'I take it you mean about making him acting sergeant? You did the right thing, boss. He'd be my first choice, and he won't let you down!'

'Anything else I should know about?'

'Yes. I've sent Luke and Jill over to that sinkhole. Did you hear about it? It was on the news this morning.'

'I got a brief introduction to it when I came in this morning, nothing more than that,' Carter replied.

'Jill called in ten minutes ago. What they found could be human remains! Jill thinks it could be a skull. She won't know for certain until she gets in there and has a look. She says it's deep, twelve feet at least.'

'Twelve feet! I can't see anyone disposing of a body that deep, can you?'

'No, I can't, but I guess it was closer to the surface, but with the collapse, it ended up in the bottom? Anyhow, I've told Jill, under no circumstances is she or Luke to go down there until it's been certified, safe! They're to wait until the Fire and Rescue Service gets there and checks it out. They'll ensure that the area and perimeter get cordoned off.'

'Are forensics in attendance?' Carter asked.

'No. Not at this stage. I asked Jill to confirm it first, just in case it turns out to be some old animal bones.'

Chapter Five

Luke Hollingsworth watched as a section of soil broke away and slid to the bottom of the hole.

PC Cotton and Best walked up behind him.' I got the farmer to shift his cows into the next field,' said Cotton. 'I told him we didn't want them getting in our way! It was he who called it in! Found it while checking his fence. He doesn't know how long it's been here. But he said it wasn't here last week.'

'Not that it matters much, I guess!' Best added.

PC Best leaned over, staring down into it, watching a blackbird search for worms in the newly fallen soils. 'The common misunderstanding,' he said, 'is to think that a sinkhole is a hole in the surface. We see the sinkhole on the ground, but the fact is, is that the hole is below the surface. Did you know that? A space like that, underground, can take hundreds or even thousands of years to form. Then, the soil from above collapses into the hole. When it collapses, you see the sinkhole on the surface. We only see the soil that's filled the hole and not the actual hole because the hole in the rock, or, in this case, the chalk, is far below. Underground streams are often the principal cause.' Pointing across the railway line to the abandoned colliery, he said. 'But remembering where we are, it could easily have been one of the underground workings that collapsed.'

'Is that right?' asked Cotton, looking at him in disbelief. 'Where the hell did you learn all that bullshit?'

'I did night school in geology. Years ago, it was,' he replied.

'Yer. Back in the stone age. C'mon, this is not safe here.' Hollingsworth said, addressing the two constables. 'Keep well back from the edge, and let's get back over the fence. The FRS should be here any minute. They'll need to tape it off.'

Gingerly, trying hard to avoid the lethal bards, the three climbed back over the fence. They went over to where Jill Richardson was leaning against the side of the patrol car. She was talking on her mobile. As they approached, she said, 'Forensic is wrapping up on another job and should be here within the hour.'

'The more I looked at it, the more it looked to me like a scull?' said Tony Best.

Cotton let out a small laugh. 'And that's your honest opinion as a geologist?' he said.

'Until we can be sure, I'd like you two to station yourselves at the gate. We're bound to get sightseers,' said Hollingsworth.

Hearing the sounds of an approaching vehicle, both turned and looked. Coming down the track was the fire and rescue truck. It drove through the gate and across the field. It stopped by the hedgerow next to where Best and Cotton's patrol car was parked. Four men climbed down from the cab. One of them, a tall red-haired man in his mid-thirties, came up to where Hollingsworth and Richardson stood. He held out his hand and introduced himself.

'Chief Officer, Brad Tomkins. FRS.'

'Luke Hollingsworth, Jill Richardson. Kingsport CID,' replied Hollingsworth.

All three shook hands. Luke was quick to notice that Jill Richardson had taken to him. He saw she held his hand a little longer than one normally would. Hollingsworth had to agree. The man certainly had a handsome quality about him. Seeing Hollingsworth looking at her, she quickly released her grip.

'It's over there,' said Hollingsworth, pointing to the trees.

'My lads will get to work. We'll soon get it cordoned off and checked out.' He nodded to them. The three went off to inspect the hole. 'I assume the property owner will get it filled in?'

'Yes. Unless he wants to turn it into a bleeding swimming pool,' muttered Hollingsworth. 'But before he does that,'

Richardson said, 'we need to know it is safe to go there. There's something we want to look at.'

'Ah. So that's why CID is here? Checking out Quatermass?' he said, looking at Richardson.

Jill Richardson responded with a chuckle. 'I hope not.'

'Ah, so you're familiar with it? The landowner! He'll need to be reminded of these regulations,' said Tomkins. 'Before he can fill it in, he must complete a full ground assessment. This has to be undertaken by a chartered geotechnical engineer or engineering geologist. Get him to contact the County Council. They'll sort him out.'

Tomkins looked over to where the three crew members negotiated the barbed wire fence that separated the field from Oxney Wood. Once over, they set to work, using trees around the hole to secure their red and white tape.

'In that case, we better look at the bottom. We need to establish if it's stable. These sinkholes can be tricky. One in France last month took a complete house. Can't have you falling through to the earth's centre now, can we?' Tomkins winked at Jill Richardson, laughed and walked off.

Once Tomkins was out of earshot, Hollingsworth said. 'Blimey, Jill, did you have to make it obvious?'

'Make what so obvious?' she asked, looking confused.

'Fireman Sam. I saw it in your eyes the moment you took his hand. Lay me down and shag me, they said.'

'Bullshit. My eyes were doing no such thing! And neither was I thinking it.' Richardson pushed a lock of hair away that had fallen across her face.

'Oh, yes! And what was so funny about that Quakermass thing that had you in stitches? What was all that about then, hey?'

'If I didn't know you any better, Luke Hollingsworth, I'd say you were jealous? Fancy him, yer self, do yer? Thinking of changing camps?' she gave him a sly look.

Hollingsworth's face flushed. 'That's not what it is, and you know it!'

'I must admit, though, he is quite good-looking.' A brief pause. For your information, smart arse, it's Quatermass, not Quakermass! It's a film,' she said. 'It's called Quatermass and the pit. They did a rerun of it recently on Foxtel. It's all about this Professor who discovers a mysterious object buried at the site of an extension to the London underground. He also found human remains over five million years old. They realise the object is, in fact, an ancient spacecraft. Quatermass believes that aliens have influenced human evolution and the development of human intelligence. They also made a tv series out of it.' She stopped talking and looked at him. 'Now we've got that sorted and out of the way. Can we please concentrate on the job at hand?'

'Well, we'll soon know if it's a spacecraft,' said Hollingsworth, turning towards the gate. 'Here comes forensics. We'll see what they have to say. I'm sure they can tell the difference between an alien and a human?'

Both started walking across to where the CSI truck was parked. Hollingsworth had only gone a short distance when he swore loudly. 'Oh, shit.' He looked down at the grass. Richardson followed his gaze. 'You just stepped in cow shit,' she laughed.

'Bloody hell. I'm not too fond of farms. The last time I was on one, I got covered in pig shit.' He did his best to clean off the shoe. Then, wiping it on a tuft of grass, he said, 'Jesus. They can teach puppies and kittens to crap in sandboxes, so why can't they teach bloody cows?'

'Because they can't build sandboxes that big. That's why.' Richardson said. She gave Hollingsworth a sorrowful look and continued walking.

As Jill Richardson approached the van, Tim Bryant, head of the CSI team, climbed out from the back of the truck. 'Ah, DC Richardson. I'm informed you have some bones for us. Is that right?'

'Yes,' she answered. 'We think so.' She pointed over in the hole's direction. 'We haven't been able to go down there yet to fully establish what they are. Fire and Rescue are checking out the bottom, ensuring it's all stable.'

One FRS team came up the ladder out of the sinkhole. He stood on the rim where, with the help of one of his teammates, he removed his safety harness. He and Tomkins stood talking for a while. After they'd finished, Tomkins climbed over the fence and strode toward Bryant, Hollingsworth and Richardson.

'It's all fine. The bottom is compacted, and you should be safe working there. The walls won't need shoring up, and the sides are hard, stable and won't fall in. You're ready! You're set to go,' he said.

'Right,' said Bryant, addressing his two colleagues, 'let's get suited up and see what we've got, shall we?' Looking at Hollingsworth and then at Richardson, he said. 'Until we establish what we've got, I suggest you two stay this side of the fence.'

'Ok, we'll pack up our gear and get on our way,' said Tomkins. He looked at his watch. 'Nicely timed, if I say so myself. Should be back just in time for lunch.' He said, 'Ok, lads, pack it up; we're done here.'

Looking over at Hollingsworth, Jill Richardson said, 'We'll need his written safety report for our records.'

'Do you need one?' replied Tim Bryant, looking over at Hollingsworth for confirmation.
Hollingsworth looked down at his shoe, checking if all the cow shit had gone. 'First, I've ever heard of it,' he replied.

'Er, yes,' Richardson said. She paused, appeared flustered, and then spoke. 'Health and safety regulations. We must have one, so if it collapses, and you get injured while in there, you can claim compo.' With that, she hurried off to catch up to Tomkins.
Satisfied his shoe was clean, Hollingsworth raised his head and watched her go. Then, smiling, he said, 'I bet you any money you like that she'll come back with his phone number?'

Chapter Six

Mike Reid read the toxicology report for a second time, closed the folder, and laid it back on the desk. He looked across the room to where James Broadbent was wrestling to open the drawer of his filing cabinet. 'So, Doc. This killed him, sodium fluoroacetate and strychnine?'

Broadbent finally won his battle with the drawer, got it opened, dropped in the file he was holding and slammed it shut. Locking it, he came back over and sat down at the desk. 'The lab had a slow morning. I was lucky and got the samples analyzed quickly. Normally I'd have to wait at least a couple of days.'

Broadbent pulled the folder towards him and opened it. He took from it a two-page printout and some photographs. He put the photos to one side and, reading from the report, said, 'Well-nourished male, aged approximately thirty-two. The only distinguishing mark is a tattoo on his right upper arm. A series of numbers, eight in all! The death occurred because of ventricular arrhythmias.' He took off his glasses and held them up to the light. Reid waited for him to explain. Broadbent took a tissue from the box, polished both lenses and put them back on. Then, looking over the rim of his glasses, he said, 'This causes abnormal heartbeats that originated in the lower heart chambers, the ventricles. These arrhythmias cause the heart to beat too fast, preventing oxygen-rich blood from circulating to the brain and body, resulting in cardiac arrest.'

'Don't they use sodium fluoroacetate as bait for wild pigs and rabbits?' asked Reid.

'Clever you. Aye, yes, they do. It was that helped your corpse off to the happy hunting grounds. If he'd had got to a hospital in time, he could, maybe, have survived. But combined with the other, the poor chap didn't stand a chance. Compound 1080 and strychnine mixed is not kind to the human body. To sum it up, that poison cocktail caused him to have a heart attack, which is a painful and nasty way to die. This was no accident. Someone spiked his booze. He was murdered.'

Reid looked down at the report Broadbent was holding open. 'This was all added to the whiskey?' he asked.

'Yes. A whiskey sample from the bottle has confirmed it.'

'The bottle has gone over to the lab boys for fingerprinting. Death by poisoning.' Reid said. He again saw, in his mind, the image of the man's body lying in the graveyard. So, not a drunk choking on his vomit, after all?'

'No. The liver showed damage. I'd say your man was a heavy drinker. There was also found a lump. I won't be a hundred per cent sure until I get the results back, but at a guess, I'd say it's cancerous.'

'How soon after drinking it would the poison have taken effect?'

'Different poisons have different effects! The poisoning symptoms normally appear between thirty minutes and three hours after exposure. Initial symptoms of this combination would typically include nausea, vomiting, abdominal pains, sweating, confusion, and agitation. Neurological effects include muscle twitching and seizures; consciousness becomes progressively impaired after a few hours, leading to a coma.'

'Those numbers tattooed on his arm?' asked Reid, looking at the photo. 'Any idea what they could be?'

'My best guess is that the man lying in the cool room is ex-military. My first instinct is to say it's his serial number; if it is, it's traceable.'

'His service number tattooed on his arm? Why would he do that? I wonder? Next, you'll be telling me he had dementia?'

'Pride. It may be to keep old memories alive. God knows. No idea! You tell me?'

Broadbent looked out of his office window at the wall clock in the dissecting room.

'But right now, it's time for a hearty lunch at the Dog and Duck. Mondays, they have a special on the menu. It's roast beef and Yorkshire pudding with homemade mint sauce. Marvelous! I never miss it. It's better than what my ex-wife used to make. But, mind you, credit where credits are due. She used to make good pork crackling.'

Broadbent got up from the desk, then went and retrieved his old hound tooth jacket with the leather patched elbows that hung on the back of the door. Slipping his arms into the sleeves, he said. 'Took her there once, hoping it would rub off.' He sighed. 'Unfortunately, it didn't. Her pud was still a disaster. If you ever go to the Dog and Duck on a Monday, you need to be there before one. Otherwise, all those greedy office sods scoff it.' He stopped by the door, turned and said, 'Would you care to join me, Inspector?'

Reid gave it a little thought, looked at his watch and said, 'Yer, why not? It beats the hell out of the canteens' egg and chips. But before I do, I'll need to call this in and let the boss in on what you've found. Murder will certainly start his week off with a bang.'

As he opened the door to leave, he saw Abbie Richards walking briskly along the corridor towards them. She was dressed in green scrubs and carrying a clipboard. Richards came from the West Indies and was Jamaican-born. She had interned with Broadbent up to a year ago. She had recently graduated, taking on the role of the second pathologist at the Kingsport General Hospital.

Abbie Richards smiled and acknowledged Reid. 'Sergeant Reid! Good morning, nice to see you again.' Reid corrected her. 'Er, it's Inspector now!' he said, smiling.

'Oh, sorry. Then I see congratulation are in order?' Then, turning to Broadbent, she asked, 'Will you be doing the autopsy on that young boy this afternoon?'

'Oh, you mean the suspected overdose? Erm, no, Abbie. Can I leave that one in your capable hands? I need to get those reports typed up for the coroner on Wednesday. Have that student assist you. What's her name? The Spanish one. The new second-year student. She's the most intelligent one of the bunch? She shows promise. At least she's not afraid of a drop of blood. I believe she once worked in an abattoir. You'll find her in the sluice room cleaning up from this morning.'

'Maria. Her name's Maria, Maria Vella, and she's Maltese, not Spanish'. Richards wrote something on her clipboard. 'Right then, I'll see you later?' She smiled, bid Reid good morning, then pushed through the swing door and headed toward the sluice room.

'There's a secret to making good Yorkshire pudding. Over lunch, I'll tell you how to make it! It's easy. Your wife will love it. I take it you are married?' Broadbent said as they walked across the parking area a few minutes later.
Reid guessed that Broadbent already knew the answer to that.

'Going steady. I believe the term is?' Reid said, patting his pocket and searching for his car keys.
Broadbent walked to the bay where his blue XF Jaguar was parked. 'Shacked up is the common term?' He turned, smiled at Reid, opened the door and got in.'C'mon, lad,' he called. 'Let's not be late!'
By the time Reid had secured his seatbelt, Broadbent was halfway across the car park.

Chapter Seven

An hour later, Reid stood on the footpath outside the Dog and Duck, reading the list of ingredients from what Broadbent had called his own 'secrete' Yorkshire pudding recipe. Maybe Emma can make some sense of it, he thought. Reid folded it in half, half again, and then slipped it into his pocket. He had to admit the Dog and Duck served an excellent lunch. He left, leaving Broadbent tucking into his second helping. Reid stood, waiting for a break in the traffic. When it came, he crossed the road to the public parking area on the other side. Walking up to his car, he pipped the lock. He was just about to open the door to get in when his phone rang. Pulling it from his pocket, he checked the name. It was Kirby! 'Marcia! You got something?'

'Yes, it's about your dead man. Mrs Daphne Webster called. She runs the White Cliffs Guest House on Upper Road. It's halfway between Dover and Saint Margarets Bay, just past the Fan Bay turnoff. I checked it out. It's a mile east of the church where his body was found. She said his name was Maurice Wilson, and he'd been staying there for the last two months. She saw his picture on the midday news.'

'Ok. By the way. This has now turned into a murder investigation.' He told her about the autopsy report. After finishing, he said, 'Marcia, now that we have a name, can you get someone on to it? See what else you can find out about him?'

'I'll get on to it myself.'

'Ok, Marcia, thanks. Oh! And let the boss know? Thanks!'

He disconnected and then put the guest house address into the map app on his iPhone. After checking the route, he Googled his destination and drove out of the car park and onto the High Street. Passing through the market square, he continued on out of town. Approaching the roundabout, he took the inside lane, then the exit that directed him to the A2.

A few minutes later, he was on his way, heading toward Dover.

****

Reid pulled off onto the side of the road some thirty minutes later, came to a stop and hit the button on the armrest, sending down the driver's window. The sign that hung from a gallows-like structure by the open gate said it welcomed long-term guests, short or overnight stays. Beneath that was a sign saying they had vacancies. He put the window back up, steered the car through the gate, and up a short, beech tree-lined drive. He brought the car to a halt in front of the building. After setting the hand brake, he opened the door and got out. The first thing he noticed was how still the air was. Not even a sea breeze stirred the leaves on the beech trees. He stood in the gravelly car park, admiring the facade. Then, he turned to look at the view. He could see the North Foreland lighthouse and, further off in the distance, the keep of Dover castle

Googling the White Cliffs revealed that the house, built during the reign of Henry the Eights, was once the property of Thomas Brooke, 8th Baron Cobham. The army had used it to train officers in the first war. Abandoned after that, it had fallen into disrepair. Then, in the thirties, it was purchased by a coal mining millionaire and converted into a guest house. However, it had always remained in the family. The three-story twenty-bedroom house stood on two acres of land surrounded by lawns and flower beds. In the entrance hall, it said, was a grand sweeping staircase leading up to the second and third floors. On the same level was a library that formally acted as a conservatory. In addition, there was a dining room, a drawing room, a TV room, and a kitchen at the back of the house.

Locking the car, he started across the car park. In front of him, four steps led up to a portico supported by four concrete columns. He walked up the steps to the stained-glass door, opened it, and walked in. The entrance hall in which he now stood was spacious. He looked around, and a stone lion stood on either side of the door. The staircase further down the hall was indeed impressive and broad. Beneath his feet lay an intricate, multi-coloured mosaic floor set in various distinct patterns. On the oak-paneled walls hung oil paintings and prints of old masters. Reid half expected to see a chambermaid dressed in a white waist apron and a white head cap walking down the staircase, carrying a coal scuttle. The place smelt old. It smelt of furniture polish and antiques. It was like he had stepped back in time.

Hearing a woman's voice, he followed the sound down the hallway to a half-opened door. Above it, the sign said, *Dining Room*. Poking his head around it, he saw two women in their late thirties, dressed in light blue smocks pushing a tea trolley between tables. They were laying out placemats, napkins and cutlery. Reid counted twelve tables. The dining room had a cosy, intimate atmosphere with oak-paneled walls, elegant chairs, and soft wool carpeting. He thought you'd need a lot of money to live this life style. One of them looked up from her task as he entered and asked. 'Can I help you?'

'I'm looking for Mrs Webster. Is she about?'
Not recognising him as a guest, she smiled and asked. 'Ah! Wanting a room, are you?'

'Er, no. I'm a police officer and just here making some enquiries.'
Both women stopped what they were doing. 'You must be here about Mr Wilson?' said the taller of the two. We didn't even know he was missing until Mrs Webster told us it was on the TV news.

'How long had he been staying here?' Reid asked.
'I'm not sure! But at least two months, maybe you'd best ask Mrs Webster about that. She owns this place. She'll know for sure. She was out in the kitchen. At least she was a minute

ago. She was with the cook, sorting out this week's dinner menu. '

'Do you know anything about him?' Reid asked, looking around the room.

The two diner ladies looked at one another, each waiting for the other to answer. They both shook their heads.

'No,' said the tall one. 'Mr Wilson was a silent man. He hardly spoke and kept himself to himself. Of course, you can speak to the other guest, but I've never seen him sitting with them at mealtimes. Have you, Marge?' she said, turning to speak to her companion. 'He always ate alone.'

'No, Fay, I never have,' Marge replied. 'As you said, he always sat by the window. Always alone. He sat over there.' She turned and pointed. Reid's eyes followed the direction of Marge's red-painted fingernail to a table on the far side of the room.

The door to the kitchen suddenly swung open, and a woman appeared carrying a clipboard. She came quickly across the carpeted floor to where the three stood. First, she looked at Reid, then at the one she called Marge, her eyes posing the question.

'He's a police officer.' Marge said. 'He came in looking for you.'

Mrs Webster was middle-aged, with brown, dull hair elaborately arranged. She had penciled-in eyebrows and prominent blue eyes and wore a dark grey, two-piece pantsuit.

'Mrs Webster? I'm Detective Inspector Mike Reid, Kingsport CID. I'm here about your call regarding Mr Wilson. You said he was a guest here? Is that correct?'

'Yes, he was. Please, call me Daphne. Mrs Webster sounds so formal. The only person who ever called me Mrs Webster was my husband.' She let out a laugh. The two dinner ladies looked at one another. Marge raised her eyebrows

'Let's go into my office, shall we? It's a bit more comfortable. We can talk there. Please follow me.'

'I take it there is no Mr Webster, then?' asked Reid.

'No. My husband passed away ten years ago. God rest his soul.'

She led Reid out of the dining room and down the hallway. As they walked, she proudly pointed out the library, reception, day, and TV room. All sat behind polished oak doors. Daphne Webster's office was across from the TV room. She opened the door. Reid followed her in. It was very much in keeping with the rest of the house, with dark wood paneling paintings and pictures. The only everyday items Reid could see were a computer, a phone, and a combination copier printer in the corner. He noticed the plate on the desk and three jam doughnuts on it. Webster saw him looking.

'One of my weaknesses, I'm afraid. I love them,' Webster said. 'I can't resist them.

'Oh. Thank you, Mrs Webster. No! I need to watch the waistline!' He patted his stomach.

'My wife keeps a close eye on it.' He smiled. 'She gets the tape measure out every time I go home.'

She looked at his waistline and then said, 'Well. Unfortunately, there's not much I can tell you about Mr Wilson,' she said, pulling the chair from under her desk and sitting down.

Before sitting down, Reid took out his phone and showed her Wilson's picture. 'Is this the same Mr Wilson you have staying here?' he asked

Daphne Webster took it from him. 'Yes, it's him. I'd recognise that scar anywhere.' Handing back his phone, she said, 'He came here two months ago. He has been no trouble and paid up every week on the dot. Nice man. Can I ask? How did he die? A heart attack? On the news, it just said he was dead?'

'We're treating it as a murder.'

With eyes wide open and pencilled eyebrows raised, she stiffened statue-like; her face frozen with shock. Then, after a few moments, it all fell back into place.

'Murdered. Oh, my God!' she cried. 'That poor man! How shocking.'

Reid waited while she composed herself, then said, 'Did he have any friends, relatives, visitors?'

'None that I know of. We ask all our long-term guests to fill out a registration form. All their details are on them. From what I recall, there was no next of kin.'

'I'll require a copy of the registration form, please.'

Pulling open a desk drawer, Daphne Webster took out a folder, thumbed through it, and handed Reid a single sheet of paper. She placed the folder back in the drawer and slid it shut.

Reid ran his eyes over the page. There was no clue where he had come from, no address or passport number. In the section for payment, there were no bank details. The box, saying residents could pay cash, had a tick against it! He carefully folded it and then slipped it into his inside jacket pocket.

He looked over her shoulder, out of the window and across the lawn. 'How long did he intend to stay here? Did he say?'

'No. Mr Wilson said he wasn't sure and had some business to attend to, and when that was done, said he'd be leaving and making himself a better lifestyle.'

'Did he say what that lifestyle was?'

'No. Mr Wilson said he was doing some research, which he hoped would bring him lots of money.'

'Nothing else?'

'No, nothing!'

'Did he have a car?'

'No, he didn't. I know for sure because when Mr Wilson arrived, it was by taxi. Mr Wilson came to me about a week later, asking where he could hire a car. I told him that Mr Pritchard, who runs the garage down in the village, has hired cars. So that's where I sent him.'

Rising from his chair, he said, 'I would like to see his room?'

'Certainly. It's on the second floor. I'll show you if you'd like to come with me.' She got out of her seat, went to a cupboard, and took out several keys.

****

Reid closed the bedroom door and stood looking around the room. A four-poster dominated the wood-paneled room. On the walls hung portraits of long-forgotten people, all in Victorian dress. There were women in ballgowns and stern-looking men in top hats. He pulled on a pair of Nitrile gloves and crossed the room to a dressing table. On it sat a bottle of cheap supermarket whiskey three-quarters full, a small medicine bottle, and a tablet box. Reid picked up the bottle and read the label. It was paroxetine and half empty. Take one daily read the instructions! He put down the bottle and then picked up the box. The label said it was Sertraline and was unopened. They both carried the name of the chemist. From the prescription, we'd be able to trace the doctor who had administered them. This is a small clue, a useful one!

He opened the top drawer and found letters, papers, and an envelope. Inside the envelope, he found photos. They were of a young woman dressed in a maid uniform standing at the bottom of some steps. Another showed her sitting on a lawn in a summer dress. After examining the papers, he went through the rest of the drawers. He found nothing but shirts, socks and underpants. He went over to the wardrobe and opened it. The clothes that hung there were cheap and smelt strongly of mothballs. He started rifling through the two suits, checking the pockets. In the trouser of one, he found a slip of paper. On it was the address and a name, Maria Jankowski! Looking down, he saw a red backpack.

He reached forward, grabbed it, then over and sat on the edge of the bed. He unzipped it and pulled out a half-empty bottle of whiskey and a beige-coloured beret with a cap badge showing a downward-pointing Excalibur wreathed in flames. Reid instantly recognised it as the badge of the Special Air Service. He sat thinking. No tablet, phone, or wallet here or at the churchyard. We know he had them, so where the hell are they? He looked around the room. The more Reid thought about it, the more it made sense! There was only one explanation! On one of those, maybe, was the clue to who killed him? His name must have been on that tablet and the phone. It had to be him that had taken them? By getting rid of the evidence, he was covering his arse. Find them, and you'll find your killer!

He walked over to the dressing table and looked into the waste bin. In it was an empty whiskey bottle. Pulling out his phone, he Googled the medication. Finally, after a few minutes of searching, he had his answer. Reid put together what little he knew about Wilson. His age was about thirty-two, and he was ex-SAS. Wilson even had his service number tattooed on his arm. This could have put him in Iraq, even Afghanistan, he thought. Had the medication been prescribed to help with PTSD? He knew post-traumatic stress disorder was a fast-growing problem among military personnel who fought in various theatres of war.

He needed to bag up what he had found, so getting up from the bed, he checked through the bathroom. Finding nothing but toiletries, he left the room and went down to his car. He returned a few minutes later with evidence bags. He filled them, left, and, locking the door behind him, slipped the key into his pocket. He'd already given Daphne Webster strict instructions that no one should enter the room until it was given police clearance.

Reid walked along the landing, past the service lift to the top of the stairs and started down. As he neared the bottom, Marge came out from the dining room.

'Inspector, I'm glad I caught you. I suddenly remembered something. I don't know if it's important, but it's about Mr Wilson. You asked if he'd had visitors. A man called to see him about three or four weeks after Mr Wilson arrived. I remember it clearly because it was Thursday, the sixteenth, two days before my birthday. I don't work on a Thursday, but I swapped with Muriel because her old mum had been hospitalised. He came in and asked me if Mr Wilson was home.'

'Did he give a name?'

'No, he didn't. So, I said I'd show him the way, but he insisted on going up alone. He said he wanted to surprise him, so I gave him Mr Wilson's room number. Later, as I was passing his door, I heard Mr Wilson. His voice was raised, and it sounded like they had a real ole' barney!'

'What were they arguing about? Did you hear?' 'No. The door was closed. But it was loud.' 'Can you describe this other man?' She paused, trying to recall. I'm not too good at remembering faces, but he was tall and well-spoken. I think he was younger than Mr Wilson. But, of course, I can't be a hundred per cent, so don't take that as gospel. He was wearing a black jacket and a bow tie!'

'Did he, by any chance, have a car? Did you notice one?' Reid asked. 'Funny you should ask me that. I asked myself that very same question. He'd left the front door open, so when I shut it and looked out into the car park, it was empty! So, I asked myself, who would bother walking out here because we'd had showers all day?'

'Did you, by any chance, see him leave?'

'No. Sorry. I was busy in the dining room.'

Looking around, Reid asked, 'Do you have security cameras? I see none here!'

'Yer we have. Or should I say, had! But a fat lot of good they were. Half the time, they don't work. Cheap and nasty is what the serviceman from Sure Safe says they were. He was out twice last week and spent more time fixing them than they did working. So, they've been taken out. We're supposed to be having a new system installed this week. State-of-the-art is what Mrs Webster calls them.'

'What time was it he came? Can you remember?'

She pulled a face as she concentrated. 'I think it was sometime between two and three!'

'Thank you, Marge, most helpful. What was your last name?'

'Tucker. Marge Tucker.'

He tucked the bags under his arm, took a card from his top pocket, handed it to her, and said. 'If you remember anything else, Marge, please call me.'

Chapter Eight

'Well, those skeletal remains are human. No doubt about it,' said Tim Bryant, pulling back the hood of his protective overalls. 'A skull and a forearm. On one side of the skull, there's a depressed fracture. It's extensive and, without doubt, would have caused the death. Going on experience, I'd say it's been there between fifteen and twenty years! From the size of the skull and looking at the teeth, we have the remains of a young adult. Teeth provide useful age information, especially in identifying subadults. I'm sticking my neck out here, but I'm guessing the age is below eighteen! Of course, I can't be a hundred per cent sure of that, so we'll have to wait and see what the anthropologist, Professor Thorp, says. She's head of forensic anthropology at Canterbury University. It's routine in cases like this!'

'I wonder if this farmer had this place back when it was buried? We need to chat with him,' Hollingsworth said to Richardson.

'Sex?' Jill Richardson asked Bryant.

'Hah! Still thinking about Fireman Sam, are we, Jill?' said Hollingsworth, smiling at her.
Richardson returned the look, saying nothing.
Bryant chose not to question Hollingsworth but said, 'From what we've got now, no. But when we find the pelvic bones, we will. There's a lot of soil to sift through. Some more of my team should be here soon to help. I'm hoping the collapse has not spread the remains too far.' He looked towards the heavens. 'They've forecast rain for later on this afternoon. The last thing we want is to have evidence washed away, and I don't fancy sifting mud. It makes the job ten times as hard.'

'While they're doing that, Jill, why don't we get a bite to eat? I'm starving.' 'Before we do anything, we must let the boss know what's happening. Tell him what we've got.'

Hollingsworth took out his phone and was about to make the call when a shout came. All three turned towards the hole. First, the head, then the shoulders, appeared at the top of the ladder. Then, finally, one of Bryant's team came into full view. One arm held high.

'Hello! Looks like he's found something!' Richardson said. The white-suited figure climbed off the ladder, successfully scaled the fence, and then walked across the grass toward them.

'What have you got, Archie?' asked Bryant.

'This,' he said. Laying in the palm of his hand was a beaded bracelet.

Tim Bryant took it from the man's hand.

'I think this answers the question about the sex of the remains. I don't see a man wearing this, do you? So, it has to belong to a female?'

'I found the sole of a shoe. Rubber with canvas still on it. Size seven, maybe ten. There are some bits of leather. There's a piece with still a plastic button on it. We also found a ring. It wasn't with the remains but in the soil just above them.'

'Any more bones?' Bryant looked to where the photographer recording the scene was emerging from the pit.

'Not as yet, no!'

'Let's get some of the muck off and see what we've got?' Bryant handed it back. The man walked off to their van.

A white four-wheel-drive Land Rover came down the track and bumped its way across the meadow towards them.

'Ah, good. Here comes the rest of the team. I'll have them start by getting a cover over the dig,' said Bryant. The Land Rover pulled up by the hedge next to the crime team's Mercedes van. At the wheel was Laura Townsend, Bryant's second in command. Het headed across to meet her.

'I'm starving,' said Hollingsworth as he and Richardson followed Bryant to the van. 'My stomach thinks my throat's been cut,'

'Make the call. Get a search underway. We're looking for a teenager, a girl, missing somewhere between fifteen and twenty years ago. As we'll be here for the rest of the day, why don't you ask Best or Cotton to go to that bakery when you've done? You know, the one we passed on the way in. Get them to grab a couple of meat pies and some drinks. I'll have orange.'

As they approached, Townsend said. 'Sounds like we have a bit of a challenge on our hands?' Then, addressing Bryant, she said, 'I've got the portable lights just in case. I'll start getting the dig covered, shall I?'

'Yer,' said Bryant, looking up at the sky. 'Make that number one priority. I don't like the look of the weather.'

Hollingsworth took Jill Richardson to one side. 'I'll go over and organise the grub, and then I think we need to talk to this farmer. What d'yer reckon?' said Hollingsworth. 'If he owned this place back then, he's got to be our number one suspect? So, let's have a word with him, shall we?'

'Luke, think about it for a moment. If you buried someone, then years later saw the skull lying at the bottom of a twelve-foot hole in the ground, what would you do? Not report it to the police, that's for sure. No! You'd keep yer mouth shut and get the hole filled in as fast as you could?'

Hollingsworth gave it some thought, then said. 'So, if he hadn't buried it, someone else had this land before him?'

'Or someone buried it without his knowledge?'

'Ok,' said Richardson, 'let's talk to him. You drive.' She tossed him the keys.

As they walked toward the car, they heard thunder in the distance.

'Looks like they're right,' said Hollingsworth. He opened the car door and got in. As Jill Richardson was fastening her seatbelt, her mobile warbled. She took it from her pocket, read the text, and smiled. She tapped out the reply and then stuck it back.

'Work?' asked Hollingsworth, looking across at her.

'No. It was my sister inviting me out to dinner.'

He put the key in the ignition and started the engine. Slipping it into gear, he headed across the field towards the gate at the end of the track. Reaching it, he stopped and put down the window.

'That farmer, did you get his detail?' he asked PC Best 'Yes, we got them,' he replied, answering Hollingsworth's question. Best bent down to peer in through the open window. 'The lot. He even wrote directions to his cottage should we need him.'

PC Mike Cotton went to their patrol car, returning a few moments later with a folded piece of paper. 'Here yer go.' He passed it through the passenger's window to Jill Richardson. She unfolded it, studied it for a short while, then said, 'Ok, Luke, up the track and left at the end. Head toward the village. Lucky you! We have to pass the bakery on the way.' Hollingsworth sped off up the track.

Chapter Nine

.

Dave Lynch stopped at the school crossing, allowing the lollipop lady in a white coat and peaked cap to see her charges safely across the road. Once across, she waved him on. He continued along George Street, past the school gates, and down the hill. There was a lot of traffic on the High Street, and he suddenly remembered why. The crossing. Of course! It was school leaving time, and mums and dads would pick up their offspring.

His next port of call was to a wine merchant in Last Lane, just off Market Square. Lynch knew the lane. It was designed in Victorian times to take horses and carts and was too narrow to park and leave a car, so he looked for an alternate place. Lynch spotted a parking space outside the Maharajah Indian restaurant halfway along the High Street. He braked, causing the driver of a large black Toyota SUV following to sound his horn. Ignoring the frustrated man, Lynch stopped and backed smoothly into the vacant space.

He got out of the car, locked it, and headed along the pavement to the pedestrian crossing. He waited for the light to turn green and then walked across. Reaching the other side of Market Square, he strolled past the barber's shop, then turned left down Last Lane. It was deserted. Nobody was around. The only sound to reach him was the traffic on High Street.

This narrow lane, now used only as a shortcut between the High Street and the East Street bus station, was once a thriving hub in this old part of the town. Now a mere shadow of what it once was. The big supermarkets had stolen the trade, and now only two shops remained open. One was John Stukey and Sons, the wine and spirit merchants, and the other, a shop selling antique books and fine prints. Across from it, boarded up, was a fish and chip shop. Yet, despite a decade of neglect, the sign above the door was still visible. As Dave

Lynch walked past, he sniffed. A trace of yesteryear still lingered.

The notice in Stukey's window said it was open from 10 am to 4 pm. Lynch pushed open the door and walked in. As he crossed the threshold, he looked at the security video screen and watched himself walk in. He looked around at the storage racks full of wine and shelves lined with spirits. The interior of the shop was tiny. He wondered how a small establishment like this could survive the competition from the town's other, much larger outlets. This little back alley shop was number four on Lynch's list of six to be checked out. From the first three, he drew a blank. They sold every other label of Johnnie Walker but not the blue one he was seeking.

He moved across the shop floor, down the aisle to the counter. On it was a push button with a note sellotaped beside it which read, *"If Unattended, Please Ring For Service."* He stabbed it with his finger. He waited a minute. Nobody appeared, so he pressed it again. This time, he held it down a little longer. There was a loud sound somewhere beneath Lynch's feet, then, to his surprise, a trap door on the floor behind the counter suddenly sprang open, and like a genie in a bottle, a man appeared. Lynch aged him. The wizened face man was well into his eighties. His white hair was wild and rambling. It looked like he'd just stuck his finger in an electrical outlet. He patted it down, setting adrift flecks of dandruff.

He looked hot and flustered. 'Sorry to keep you waiting, sir. I was down in the cellar checking the monthly stock order and cleaning. My brother Micheal handles that normally, but he has a hospital appointment this afternoon. It was the only day he could get.'

Lynch could not help but notice the framed document fixed on the wall behind the counter. It was a Royal Warrant, and it bore the coat of arms of Prince Albert. It was dated 1842. Three years after his marriage to Queen Victoria. Beneath that is a picture of a man in a frock coat and top hat. He was holding a scroll. The man saw Lynch looking.

'That's my great-great-grandfather, John Stukey. The business was started by him. That was taken the day he received the warrant.' He looked up at the wall, sighed and said, 'Sadly, no longer active.'

Lynch wasn't sure which one the man was referring to! The warrant or the great-great-grandfather? It had to be both!

'Umm, I was wondering if you could help me. Do you, by any chance, stock Johnnie Walker Blue Label?'

The man turned to Lynch. 'Yes, sir, we do. We only order a small amount. Being expensive, it only goes to very selective customers, such as upmarket hotels and restaurants. We keep a few on hand, though. How many would sir like?'

'None.' Lynch replied. 'I'm Acting Detective Sergeant Lynch. Kingsport CID.' He showed his identity.

The wine merchant's expression changed. He stood there, his brow creased.

Lynch explained to the man what he wanted and then showed him the photo of Wilson.

'No, err, sergeant. I've never seen that man here in my shop.' He handed it back across the counter to Lynch. 'He's brought nothing from me. My last sale went to Ripton Hall. His Lordship has a case of it. It's a standing order. I can even tell you the date it was sent out. It was picked up today, this morning. Normally we deliver, but today his Lordship's son, Peter, came in and collected it. Said he was in town on business. Good customer, his lordship. He always pays on time.'

After Lynch was given a list of the restaurants and hotels to which Stukey had supplied the whiskey, he thanked him and headed for the door. Lynch walked out and made his way back up the lane to the High Street where he'd left his car. As he drew level with the bookshop, two teenagers came toward him. The girl's hairstyle was a protest against the establishment. It was cut into a Mohawk. It stood about four inches high and was dyed yellow, red, and mauve. Rings dangled from each of her ear lobes and one through the nose. The large lace-up boots and skin-tight jeans she wore made her look menacing.

Her companion, a boy, looked no better. He was dressed in a hoodie and wore tattered jeans. The man wore rings. He had one in each ear and one through his bottom lip. Beneath the hood, his long ginger hair hung down over his forehead, partly hiding his face. How old were they, Lynch thought, nineteen, twenty? As they drew level, the girl and Lynch's eyes momentarily met. The two continued down the lane and entered the shop.

Lynch watched. He hurried back and watched them through the window. Inside, he saw them glance swiftly around and disappear from view behind one of the wine racks. Lynch was instantly on alert. This was not their usual haunt! Stukey's was not the place that stocked casks of wine and six-packs. His first thought was that they were shoplifters! Lynch moved to where he could watch without being seen, took out his phone, and called for backup. He was sure he had seen her before.

He watched as the pair came back into view and moved toward the counter where the Stukey was standing. The boy held something down at his side. Lynch couldn't see what it was. When they got to the counter, the boy raised his arm, revealing what he was hiding. A knife. A large kitchen knife. The girl started shouting at Stukey. The boy joined in, waving the knife around, slicing it through the air, and threatening him. Stukey staggered backwards in surprise. Fearing for the man's life, Lynch moved fast. He pushed open the door and rushed into the shop.

The boy turned and pointed the knife toward him. Lynch held up one hand, calling him to stop. In the other, Lynch held his ID. 'I'm a police officer. Put the knife down, son. You don't want to hurt anybody.' All the time Lynch talked, he'd been moving slowly towards the counter. Finally, he stopped. 'I've already called for backup, and they'll be here any minute. Put the knife down, step back and get on your knees. Come on, you two, be sensible. Let's not make things any worse.'

Old Mr Stukey, who had been standing, scared and white-faced, groaned, grabbed at his chest and slumped to the floor.

'He needs help,' Lynch said. 'he's having a heart attack. I'm calling for an ambulance.' Lynch went for his phone. While Lynch was distracted, the girl yelled, 'Fuck this, Jake! I'm out of here.' She turned and ran to the far side of the shop. Lynch had another feeling of recognition. That girl! He was sure he'd seen her before! She hit a tall display rack in her dash for the door, toppling it. Bottles hit the ground and shattered, spilling red wine across the floor. From where Lynch stood, he had no way of stopping her. All he could do was watch. She was much closer to the door than he was. In a flash, she was out through it and running hell for leather along the lane.

With the way now blocked by the fallen wine rack, there was only one way for the boy to go, straight past Lynch. The boy's eyes were glazed, staring. He stood defiantly, swearing at Lynch. Then, with the knife firmly clasped in his hand, he yelled to Lynch to move away. Lynch knew an addict when he saw one! What was this one on, ice, coke? Lynch knew the boy would run for it if he went to the old man's aid. So, moving to one side, he tried to look at the old man lying behind the counter, but all Lynch could see were his feet.

Lynch turned and faced his aggressor. 'C'mon, Jake, do the smart thing. Please give it up! Your girlfriend's gone and left you to it.' Lynch gestured with his head to where the old man was lying. 'If he dies, it'll be down to you. You don't want that, do you? I need to call for an ambulance.'
The boy lunged with the knife. 'Fuck you. Let me pass, and then you can help the old man?'

How long ago was it since Lynch had called for backup? It felt like an age, but Lynch knew only minutes had passed. What was the average emergency response time these days, ten or fifteen minutes? Where the bloody hell were they?

Lynch's decision was obvious. He knew what he had to do! He had no choice. The older man's life was more important, and he had to let the boy go. The girl was distinctive and could be picked up. later

'Okay. Go,' said Lynch. He moved, allowing the boy to pass. The boy moved cautiously forward, the knife pointing directly at Lynch. It's times like this that Lynch wished he'd been wearing a stab vest! As the boy neared, Lynch moved closer to the counter. Thinking he was about to be jumped by Lynch, the boy rushed and lashed out at Lynch with the knife. Trapped with his back against the counter, Lynch reacted by grabbing the boy's arm, but he tore it free. With his other hand, the boy pulled Lynch toward him. Lynch felt a burning pain in his side. Latching on to the boy's hood, he pulled it back. Lynch then kicked him hard, causing him to lose balance. Grabbing at the wrist, Lynch pushed back hard on the boy's hand. There was a sickening crack. The boy screamed, dropped the knife, and fell to the floor, whimpering. 'You bastard,' he said, spitting out the words, 'you've broken it. Fuck you.'
Panting hard, Lynch bent and retrieved the knife. He groaned, wincing as he stood upright. The pain in his side hurt like hell. Pulling aside his jacket, he examined the wound. He pulled up his blood-soaked shirt, and above the waistband was a cut about two inches long.

At that moment, the shop door opened, and in came a paramedic. He looked around, spotted Lynch propped up against the counter and said. 'What's the emergency?'
'It's over here. The old man behind the counter he's had a heart attack.'

Another medic, a female, came in behind him. Pushing her partner to one side, she hurried in. Then, stepping over the boy, she went around behind the counter. 'I think we'll need a second unit here,' she said to her companion. 'I'll see to this one. You see to the others?'

Lynch's attacker still lay curled up on the floor, whimpering. Lynch identified himself to the medic, then said, 'He's got a broken wrist, and I've been bloody well stabbed,' He leaned against the counter, hand pressed up against his side.

After examining the boy, who was now shackled to a wine rack by one hand, the medic said,' Clean break. He'll survive.' To Lynch, he said, 'Let's look at you first, shall we?' He placed his medical bag on the counter.

Tony Best and partner PC Reg Stanton appeared in the doorway. The two uniformed constables took in the scene. Stanton stared at the red wine spread across the floor in the far aisle. 'Shit! My God. That's not blood, is it?'

Chapter Ten

'The medication should kick in soon, and it'll help with the pain,' said the paramedic.

'Yer. I can feel it. It's working already,' replied Lynch.

'The incision's not too deep. It's not a serious wound. It looks worse than it is. You'll be going to need a few stitches, though. You'll be left with a scar! First, we must get this man away to the Coronary Care Unit. We'll get you, and the boy transported back to Kingsport General as soon as the second unit arrives. They shouldn't be too long!'

'How is he?' Lynch asked the female medic.

Stukey lay there, his eyes open, a mobile ESG unit attached to his chest. He was conscious. The medic started removing the electrodes.

'It's okay. You're going to be fine.' She patted the man's hand. 'We'll soon have you out of here and off to the hospital.' She rechecked his blood pressure. 'I'm just going to put some saline in you now because your blood pressure is dropping. It's nothing to worry about, John. You just lay still and relax.'

Lynch turned and spoke to PC Stanton. 'You say you know this boy?' he asked.

'Yer, we've run across him a few times, haven't we, Tone?'

'Yes,' replied Tony Best. 'Stop and search. Mostly drug-related. Suspicion of dealing. Minor offences. He must have been on another planet to do this. His name is Jake Upton. You say there was a girl?'

'Yes, look at the security video. See if any of you recognise that girl?'

Stanton went behind the counter and disappeared into the back room.

Lynch looked at PC Best. 'One of you had better come with us in the ambulance. Stay with him all the time. I don't want him out of your sight.'

'We've been over at that sinkhole all shift. We were at the end of our shift and were on our way back when the call went out. So, we came straight here,' said Best.

The word was work, but you won't get paid for it. Remembering the overtime restraints, Lynch said, 'Okay. As soon as we get to the hospital, I'll have someone on the late shift babysit! I'll need someone here at the shop as well.'

Two more medics came into the shop. They greeted their colleagues. After being briefed by the first response team, they helped lift John Stukey onto the trolley bed. Lynch walked over to it. The old boy looked pale.

Lynch reassured him. 'Don't worry about the shop, John. I'll get someone here for when your brother returns. I'll get them to drive him over.' Stukey nodded, smiled, and then closed his eyes.

That done, they wheeled him out of the shop to the waiting ambulance at the end of the lane.

Lynch took out his mobile. He requested that two PCs be sent. One was for the shop to wait for the brother's arrival, and the other to guard Upton at the hospital. As Lynch placed the phone back in his pocket, Reg Stanton came out from the backroom. 'Hey, Tony. Come and look at this, will yer? See what you reckon?'

Lynch, hand pressed against his wound, followed PC Best through the door and into the back room.

Stanton pulled up a chair for Lynch, sat down and set the recorder playing. They watched.

'Who does she remind you of?' asked Stanton.

Best shook his head. 'No. I can't say she rings any bells with me.'

Stanton fast-forwarded the recording, then paused it. The girl's face was now looking directly into the camera.

'The hair?' said Stanton.

'What about it?' replied Best. 'It's horrible.'

'Yer, but apart from that. Picture her bald. No hair, a skinhead.'

It took a few moments for it to sink in. Then, after forming a mental picture, Best began clicking his thumb and finger together. 'Yer, yer. What's her name, er…?'

It was Lynch who provided the answer.

'Yer, of course, it is. Now I remember. Her name's Carol Foreman. She and her boyfriend, Arthur Fisher, tried setting fire to a mosque a while ago. He was also done for credit card theft. Stole it and booked a dirty weekend,' Lynch said.

'Middle name. Mary, aka "Crazy Carol." Yes, he thought. She looked familiar. It was the hair that threw me. Yep, that's her, alright!

'I wasn't sure, but that's who she reminded me of,' replied Stanton.

'She must have given old Fisher the flick and taken up with this Upton character, said Best. 'Now I remember. Both were given two hundred hours of community service.'

The medic popped his head in through the door. 'Ready to roll when you are!'

'Until relived, one of you with me, one stays here. You can toss for it.' said Lynch.

Chapter Eleven

Two paramedics came along the corridor, one pushing a wheelchair. In it, a heavily pregnant woman. She was panting, and her face was distorted and covered in sweat. One paramedic was holding her hand. Carter stood aside, allowing them to pass. He disliked hospitals. No matter how often he came here, it reminded him of his late wife, June, and her struggle with cancer. To Carter, a hospital corridor was just a delivery route. It was a thoroughfare for ambulance crews, with patients as parcels. The corridor had the same personality and looked like the rest of the hospital. The floor was slate grey, the walls cream, and the ceiling made from polystyrene squares.

Like the police, money and human resources for the hospital were also scarce. Cutbacks were everywhere. Nowhere was the chronic underfunding more apparent than in the corridors of hospitals. Carter walked past four patients on trolleys, some tended by anxious relatives and some alone. Each of them lies on their back, strapped in. A doctor in green scrubs, her black hair tied low in a ponytail, leaned over a trolley, talking to the man lying on it. His right arm was heavily bandaged.

Leaving the Emergency Department, Carter headed down the corridor towards the exit. He walked past the nurse's station, past the reception area, and a minute later, found himself out in the ambulance drop zone. Next to an ambulance, a TV crew was interviewing a man. Carter recognised the elderly gentleman in front of the camera. Earlier, he'd introduced himself to Carter as Micheal, John Stukey's younger brother, but only by a year.

Looking at his watch, Carter saw it had just gone six and guessed that the interview was going live on KMTV. Unfortunately, the woman holding the mike saw Carter. Not wanting to be interviewed, Carter picked up the pace and hurried to his car. As he reached it, his phone rang. It was

Marcia Kirby. He listened. 'Good idea. I could do with one. I'll be there in ten.' Carter made a brief call telling Christine he would be a bit late, said he loved her, then sticking the phone back into his pocket, drove out of the car park and headed off to town and the Black Bull.

****

Some ten minutes later, Carter walked into the public bar and looked around. There weren't many drinkers in. If they'd had any sense, they'd all be home now, having dinner and watching television. It's where I should be, he thought. In the corner, two older men were playing dominoes. It was a game Carter could never see the sense of. The only other patrons, a group of six, occupied the table by the window. Carter loosened his tie and walked over to the bar. Overhearing part of the conversation about exams as he passed, he picked them out as students from the nearby University. He'd seen their frugal spending before, six half-pints and a packet of crisps between them.

The nightly news was on the big screen above the bar. With his back to Carter, George Sutton stood watching it. He didn't notice Carter standing there until the news item finished. He turned.

'Bob, I saw it earlier on the news, the attack. How's Lynch?' said the Black Bear's landlord. 'The news said it was a couple of kids who did it? Boy and a girl?'

'I've just been over at the hospital. Dave is okay, George. Nothing that a band-aid and a good night's sleep won't fix. E's tough. Yer, kids. We got the boy. The girl legged it.'

'Do yer want yer usual, Bob?' Sutton asked.

'Yer. Make it a pint, will yer, George? I need it. Human remains in a sinkhole, a murder and a stabbing, and it's only Monday!'

'Yer. I heard about that sinkhole. Wally Short from the Advertiser was in lunchtime.' Sutton pulled Carter's pint and placed it on the bar. 'A murder? Who was it?'

Carter turned, making sure those at the nearby table couldn't overhear. 'It was that fellow they found in the graveyard on Saturday. We got a name, Wilson. Maurice Wilson. Ring any bells?'

'Yer, I saw the appeal. I can't say I've come across the name, though! But the rumor was he choked on his puke?' Sutton said, 'What did he die of?'

Not going into the full details, Carter just said. 'Poisoned. Someone nobbled his drink. JW Blue Label. '

'Waste of a good drop. Should have chosen a cheaper brand!' replied Sutton. 'If I hear of anything, I'll let you know!'

Carter never worried about sharing information with Sutton because Sutton always kept his ear to the ground, and George Sutton was a retired Inspector. So whatever Carter told Sutton stayed with Sutton! Knowing that it was a watering hole for the local plod, it automatically became a no-go area for the criminal fraternity. The Saracen's Head was much more to their liking. Spit and sawdust.

'Are the others in?' asked Carter.

Sutton took the tea towel from over his shoulder and wiped the bar top. Then he nodded his head toward the other bar. 'In there! Came in about a quarter of an hour ago.'

'Cheers, George! My regards to the misses.'

Carter picked up his pint and walked through into the Sportsman's bar. Mike Reid and Marcia Kirby were in a booth by the window, Reid with a pint and Kirby nursing a gin and tonic. Seeing Carter, Reid slid along the seat, making room for him.

'How's Dave?' Kirby asked, 'Is he okay?'

Carter sat, but before answering, he raised the glass to his lips and took a mouthful. Then, placing it back on the table, he ran his hand across his mouth.

'Ah, that tastes good. Er, yer, Dave. Apart from him being sore, he's fine. They've sown him up and sent him home with four stitches. The Doc told him to take things easy for a week and avoid bending. No physical activities or exercises.'

'No physical activities,' repeated Kirby. She looked across at Carter and laughed. 'Bet that'll please Maggie?'

For a moment, Carter didn't pick up on the meaning. Eventually, he clicked. 'Oh, yes. That!'

'So, what's the story with Dave? He walked straight into that place while the holdup was taking place. Was that it?' said Kirby. She leant forward, placing both arms on the table. Carter took another mouthful of his beer and told them about going to the hospital and what Lynch told him had happened.

After Carter had finished explaining, Reid said. 'Well, I guess we've all been in that position some time, or rather. What do you do in that kind of situation? Wait for backup or to go to the rescue? Seeing a life-threatening situation unfolding before him, Dave went in. I'm just glad he wasn't seriously injured. It could have been worse!'

'And what about the girl, Foreman? We saw her on the news. Any sign of her yet?' asked Kirby.

Carter shook his head. 'Nothing yet.' He looked up at the tv screen over on the far wall. The news was on, but the sound was muted. The camera zoomed in on the tree area where the sinkhole lay. It then shifted to the forensics van, the surrounding activity, and then back to the entrance to the field guarded by a patrol car. The captions below were too small for Carter to read.

Carter's eyes moved to the door. Luke Hollingsworth had just walked in. Glass in one hand, a packet of pork scratchings in the other. When Carter turned his attention to the tv, the weather girl was standing there, pointing to a low depression coming in off the North Sea. Hollingsworth took a seat next to Kirby.

'I'm only staying for this half, and then I'm off home. I'm starving. All I've had to eat all day is one meat pie! That's not enough to feed a sparrow! He looked around at the others. Tell me. What happened? Is Dave okay?'

For five minutes, Carter explained what had happened in the wine merchants.

Having expected Richardson to walk in with Hollingsworth, Kirby asked, 'Where's Jill?'

'Oh! Jill! She had to get home and get herself ready. She's going to meet her sister for dinner.'

Hollingsworth broke open the packet, picked out a large piece of pork, popped it into his mouth and started crunching. Then, as an afterthought, he offered the packet to the others. They declined, shaking their heads.

Kirby, surprised, looked across the table at Carter, then at Reid. 'Sister? I understood Jill was an only child?'

Carter nodded. 'Yer, as far as I know, she is.'

Hollingsworth suddenly recalled the long handshake and how Richardson had rushed off to get the safety report. He stopped crunching. 'Shit. I was right. She got his bleeding phone number and got a date as well! Bloody hell! Fireman Sam! Would you believe it?'

Those around the table gave strange looks; all of them directed at

Hollingsworth. 'Don't ask, he said.'

Chapter Twelve

Tuesday

Closing the door behind him, Carter left his office and headed towards the Incident Briefing room. Everyone had already gathered there, waiting. He went to the whiteboard, cleaned away notes from a previous briefing, and then casually tossed the eraser on the table.

Carter looked around before saying, 'Two major investigations, and we're one down. Dave Lynch will be away for at least seven days. This morning he will be on a direct video link from home to court. And before you ask, Carol Foreman is still out there. The CPS has assured me that with Jake Upton's record, he won't get bail. He'll be remanded. One more thing! I've just had the Commander on the line. She wants both wrapped up as quickly as possible and is prepared to bring in a second team to take over one investigation. I told her we'd handle it. It was a fight to keep them, so don't let me down. As we're thin on the ground, I will be with you, not sitting on my arse behind the desk. Does anyone have questions?'

With a bacon sandwich in one hand and a cup of coffee in the other, Hollingsworth asked, 'Does wrapped up quickly mean we get to do overtime?'
Before Carter could answer, Jill Richardson, in an irritated voice, called to him, saying, 'No, Luke. It means you must spend more time working and less time bloody eating.'
It brought a few laughs.
'So, who got out of bed on the wrong side this morning? Or should I say, got out of the wrong bed this morning?'
'What are you on about? Piss off, Luke.'
'Did he show you his hosepipe?'
'Luke, shut it. What the hell is wrong with you this morning? What are you on about?'
Reid and Turner exchanged looks. A brief silence.

Carter banged his hand down on the table. 'Okay, you two, break it up. Whatever's going on between the pair of you, please stop it. You're acting like a pair of kids?'

'Sorry, boss. Just having a bit of a joke.' said Hollingsworth.

Carter turned his attention to Mike Reid. 'Anymore on Wilson?' he asked.

Reid picked up his coffee. Feeling the outside of the mug was cold, he placed it back on the table. 'After I left White Cliffs, I spoke to the garage owner. He confirmed a car was hired by Wilson. One time, Wilson told him he was going to the Public Record Office in Maidstone. I checked with them, and they identified him from his picture. They told me he'd been there and asked for a copy of a death certificate for a Maria Jankowski. I am pretty sure Maria Jankowski is the woman in those photos?' he said, pointing to them on the workboard. He paused, checked his notes, and then continued. 'Wilson wanted a birth certificate, but they told him he'd have to apply to the General Register Office in Southport. He was told to email them and get an application form.' He looked over at Carter. 'I've been through all Wilson's stuff, and there's no sign of any certificates.'

Reid stood and walked over to the work board. 'Another thing I found was that while he was staying at the guest house, he had a visitor, a man. A staff member overheard both men arguing in Wilson's room on Thursday afternoon, two days before he was found dead.'

'What about a description? Did you get one? Do you think he had anything to do with his death?' asked Carter.

Reid nodded. 'He was deliberately trying to conceal his identity. I think this is the man we should talk to. He holds the answer. I believe he even left his car outside the walls so it wouldn't be seen. There were signs that a car was on the verge.'

Hollingsworth asked the question. 'Why leave the car outside but walk in and show your face? It makes little sense?'

Reid had the answer. 'Faces can be hard to describe. Even our witness, feet away from him, gave a vague description. But a car, its colour, shape. They stand out, and that is the case here. The car is recognisable; maybe it's a delivery van with a name on it?'

'What description have we got of him?' Marcia Kirby asked.

'Only one of the staff members saw him. She described him as tall and well-spoken, wearing a black jacket and a bow tie! Not much to go on. Unfortunately, the security cameras weren't working at the time of his visit.'

'I think we may have to find this man,' said Hollingsworth. 'He might throw some light on it?'

'What about that tattoo on Wilson's arm? Did you get anywhere with that?' asked DC Turner.

'No. That's something you can do, Bill. Get on to the Army, and see if you can get his service records.

Carter looked across the room to where Luke Hollingsworth sat, examining the innards of his sandwich.

'Luke! Jill! What's happening with the Oxney site?' Richardson and Hollingsworth looked at each other. Then, finally, Richardson nodded, letting Hollingsworth do all the talking.

'They should finish clearing the site later this afternoon. All the remains have been taken down to the forensic lab in Canterbury for examination by Professor Thorp. Depending on how busy they are, Tim said it could be two to three days before we get anything back! He said Professor Thorp would contact you sometime today. We tried to have a word with John Preston, the farmer, yesterday, but he wasn't around, so I went to Woolage first thing this morning to see him.' Holding up the bacon sandwich, he looked over to Richardson.'Hence the late breakfast.'

Richardson smiled. 'I stand rebuked. I take back all I said. '

Hollingsworth ignored the remark and continued. 'I got the history of the place, and Preston only manages the farm and has done so for the last five years. He lives in the village. The actual owner of the farm is a lawyer by the name of Galbraith. Preston referred to him as a gentleman farmer. He said he lives in London and comes out only after dark. Or whatever the hell that means. I'll need to dig more to find out who had it before him.'

'Five years. So, Preston is no longer the number one suspect on your list, Luke?' asked Richardson.

'Yes.' admitted Hollingsworth.

'Okay. Is there anything else I should know?' asked Carter, looking slowly around the table. Heads shook. 'Okay. Nothing else? Good. In that case, let's get back to work.'

They all headed for the door. Richardson and Hollingsworth were the last ones through. As they walked into the hallway, Hollingsworth stopped, turned to Richardson and said, 'Sorry Jill, I was bang out-of-order saying what I did back there!'

'That's okay, Luke. I make allowances for those dying of starvation!' She walked quickly off up the hallway. Hollingsworth struggled hard to keep up. Richardson stopped in front of the door of the CID office, spun around, and said. 'And just so you know, for future reference, my mother got married last year for a second time. So not only do I now have a stepfather but also a half-sister!' Richardson walked through the door and over to her workspace. 'Her name is Marion, not Fireman Sam!'
Hollingsworth followed her across the room and dropped into his chair. Then, lifting his eyes to the ceiling, he said to himself. 'Shit! Did I get that wrong?'

Chapter Thirteen

After checking out the crime report, Bill Turner put down the phone, got up from his seat, went across the room to Reid's office, tapped on the door, and walked in.

'Two weeks before his death, Maurice Wilson was involved in an incident.'

Reid looked at Turner. 'What kind of incident?'

'On Tuesday the fourteenth at three twenty, dispatch received a call from Ripton Hall, the home of Lord Maurice Ripton, complaining about a man causing a disturbance. He was abusive, assaulted a gardener, and insisted he talk to Lord Ripton. When he refused to leave, the police were called. Ambrose and Tanner attended. They said in the report that he smelt of drink. Wilson had a car, so they breathalysed him. He passed. The Hall insisted no charges be laid. They took his details, gave him a caution and sent him on his way.'

'Why was Wilson there? Did they say?' said Reid.

'No. There's nothing here in the report about it!'

'I think it's time we paid his lordship a visit and found out what that was all about?'

'You be wasting your time there, I'm afraid, 'said Turner. 'Lord Ripton speaks to no one. He hasn't done so for some time. He had a stroke. It left him incapacitated, semi-paralysed, and in a wheelchair. He has a full-time carer. He can't even feed himself, so they say! There is a son, Peter. He would be the one to talk to because he's running it all now. He might throw some light on it! There is no Lady Ripton. She's listed as deceased.'

'Ripton! That's the second time this week I've heard that name. So, Lord Ripton, just who is he?' Reid said.

'Never heard of him. So I had to look him up myself in Debrett's Peerage, Who's Who and Google!' said Turner. 'His official title is Viscount. He's got a large estate just outside of Whitstable. It's called Ripton Park, about thirty minutes from here! Runs fallow deer and owns three farms, two TV stations, four newspapers, a shipping line, and a string of properties in Knightsbridge. The average property price of a home in that neighborhood is nearly three and a half million quid. All that money, and he ends up in a bleeding wheelchair! A fat lot of good that's done him?'

'Whitstable, Aye? That's about a forty-five-minute drive from White Cliffs? Okay, Bill, excellent work. Leave it with me, and I'll get on to it. One more job for you. Maria Jankowski! Check with immigration, and see what you can find out about her, will you? I'd like to know more about this woman and why Wilson had her photos?'

'Right. I'm on to it. Oh! one other thing. The address on that piece of paper you found in Wilson's room. Turns out it's a convent run by Catholic nuns, the Sisters of St Paul! It's outside Sevenoaks Ivy Hatch! The place was once an orphanage and hospital for the sick and poor but closed in '89. So, it's now just a convent!'

'Okay, Bill, thanks.' Turner left, shutting the door behind him.

Reid sat there for some time, thinking about what Turner had just told him. The more Reid thought about it, the more convinced he was that Wilson was looking for a relative. A sister! A brother! Who knows?

Reid's phone rang. He reached across and picked it up.

'CID, Reid.'

'Inspector Reid. Congratulations on your promotion.' Straight away, Reid recognised the Cornish accent. 'Sergeant Penrose. Dave! How are you? How're things in Dover?'

'Wet one minute, raining the next,' he replied.

Reid laughed. 'Sergeant, Dave. What can I do for you?'

'We had a break-in on our patch last night. So, I think it's one you might be interested in?'

Puzzled, Reid asked, 'Why's that?'

'I believe you came here to White Cliffs yesterday inquiring into the death of Maurice Wilson?'

'Yer. I was there. Why? You said, here! Are you at White Cliffs now?' Reid could hear seagulls.

'I am. I'm outside in the car park, about to head back to town.'

'What's happened?'

'Sometime between ten last night and five this morning, someone broke into White Cliffs and ransacked Wilson's room.'

'An inside job? A resident, maybe?' suggested Reid.

'No.' replied Penrose. *'The back door to the kitchen was forced. Wilson's door was jemmied, and the room searched. Nobody heard or saw a thing. I thought maybe you might know what the intruder was after. Any ideas?'*

There was a long pause before Reid answered. 'No, I don't. I went through his room with a fine-tooth comb, taking away some documents and photos. Apart from some clothes in the wardrobe and the normal toiletries, that's all there was. One thing: he had a visitor shortly before he was killed. I think he may have had something to do with it!'

'I've got forensics checking for prints,' said Penrose. Unfortunately, there's no CCTV. It's not working.

'What about local street cameras?'

'No. Not in this neck of the woods. Oh, one more thing. Mrs Webster would like to know when she can have the room back?'

'Okay. Tell Webster I'll call her at the end of the week. I still might need to go back there.'

'Okay. If I come across anything, I'll let you know. Oh. Just one more thing. Will you tell Sergeant Kirby it's now official? She'll know what I mean!'

'Okay, thanks, sergeant, I'll tell her. Keep in touch!' Reid replaced the handset. He looked through the glass wall to see if Marcia Kirby was about. She was at the copying machine. Reid got up, stuck his head out the door, and called to her, 'Marcia! You got a minute?' He returned to his seat.

Kirby gathered up the material lying on the copier and entered the office.

Reid tapped the file lying on the desk. 'Fresh developments in the Wilson enquiry.' Reid told Kirby what Bill Turner had found out about the break-in at White Cliffs.

'Marcia, I thought of sending a DC, but as this inquiry involves the lorded gentry, I think a higher rank is called for. So, the two of us should go? Oh, one more thing, I nearly forgot! Sergeant Penrose said to tell you it's now official. He said you'd know what he was talking about?' Reid looked at Kirby, his face full of curiosity.

'Yes, I do.' She smiled. 'Dave told me on Sunday, and I said nothing because it wasn't official. Now it's official, I can tell you. Dave's being promoted. He'll be taking over from DI Marchbanks when he retires. That's why he turned down the DCI's offer. If he moved to Kingsport from Dover, he would have missed out.'

Reid nodded. 'Well, when you next talk to him, pass on my congratulations.'

Chapter Fourteen

Carter moved the cursor, ticked the box, accepted the conference invitation, and waited. A few seconds later, the screen on the wall came to life. Carter now saw the picture on the screen of a workbench. Gathered around it were several people in white crime scene suites. Suddenly the head and shoulders of Diana Thorp appeared, filling the big screen.

'Professor. Nice to see you again,' said Carter. Diana Thorp, Professor of Forensic Anthropology at Canterbury University, smiled. '*And you, Chief Inspector.*' she said.'

'I assume this call is about those remains? DC Hollingsworth said you'd be calling! I thought he meant on the phone.'

There was a noise like someone had dropped something. Professor Thorp turned to see what it was. She turned back to face Carter. '*Yes. As you can see behind me, we're on to it now. I can tell you it's a young woman, five foot five, approximately sixteen years of age. There is a severe fracture to the right side of the skull. That would have caused her death. I'd say she's been in the ground for about fifteen to twenty years. But don't hold me to it because we still have a few more tests to do. We should have a complete DNA result later today. DNA is a powerful tool for telling us who people are, even when they can no longer tell us themselves.*'

'Will you have any problems getting DNA?' Carter asked her.

'*No problem. We can even extract DNA from thousand-year-old skeletons, given the right conditions! For example, DNA was found in the remains of a man who died ten million years ago in the Cheddar Gorge. Have you heard of him?*'

Carter had. 'Yer, I have. At school. I can't say I took much notice of it, though! Anthropology was not part of the school curriculum back then!' He managed a smile.

Carter heard laughter. Was it his joke being laughed at or someone at the examination table? Thorp turned to check what was happening behind her. Thorp said something to those behind her, but it was muffled. Carter couldn't hear what she said. Finally, she turned, facing the screen. *'Thanks to this DNA, even though he's been dead for 10,000 years, we now know that this long-dead early man, called Cheddar Man, had dark hair, skin, and blue eyes!'*

The first recorded "English man" a thousand years ago had blue eyes, black skin and dark hair. Skin didn't become paler until later. So perhaps, as we think of racism, we can let those facts sink in. Black is the original skin colour of this island. We are all related and much more closely than modern culture teaches us. Amazing, right?

Carter tried his best to sound impressed. 'Bloody hell yer. Real amazing!'

She said, *'Even more amazingly, scientists established a family link between Cheddar Man and a high school teacher who lived in Somerset!'*

'Now, that is something,' said Carter.

'The speed of DNA decay depends on a lot of factors. In particular, the breakdown of DNA is sped up by heat, sunlight, water, and even microbes. Even if these conditions aren't met, we should still get mitochondrial DNA. Mitochondrial DNA is passed down from a mother to her children. Each cell in your body has two copies of most of your DNA… but there are hundreds to thousands of copies of mitochondrial DNA. That's a lot of mitochondrial DNA!' she emphasised every syllable. *'Since there's more of it, we have a higher chance of finding some that haven't been degraded. DNA in old skeletons is best preserved in a bit of bone inside the skull, called the petrous bone, part of the temporal bone. That is where we will find our DNA and, hopefully, a lead to finding her family?'*

'Okay, that's good news,' said Carter

'Have you seen this bracelet and other items from the site yet? Tim said he's got thirty of them.' Thorp asked.

'No, Professor, I haven't. Tim was supposed to send over photos of everything they found this morning.' Carter looked up at the clock. Nine-thirty. 'I'm still waiting!'

'Okay then, Chief Inspector. I'll get back to it. I just thought it best to keep you updated, and I'll be in touch when we get the results. You have a good day!'

'You to Professor, and thanks for the update.' The screen went blank.

Chapter Fifteen

There was very little traffic on the road, and they made good time. Following the directions on the screen, Marcia Kirby turned off the A229 onto the slip road. Turning right, she steered the black Skoda Octavia across the overpass spanning the Thanet Way, then headed down the narrow road towards the village of Hernhill. After a few miles of twists and turns and a couple of farms later, Reid spotted it. 'Over there! There it is.' He pointed at it through the windscreen. It was barely visible through the trees. 'There! That big place. That has to be it? Do you see it?'
Kirby slowed the car. 'Yer, I see it.'

A hundred yards further on, the hedgerow was replaced by a twelve-foot high wall, the top covered in broken glass and strands of barbed wire.

'All that to keep deer in?' Kirby remarked, looking up at it.

'I'd say more likely it's keeping people out,' Reid replied. Kirby pulled in and stopped at the gatehouse, unable to proceed past the tall metal gates that graced the entryway. On each was fixed the family crest. Above, a security camera, a spy in the sky, stared down at them from on top of the wall. Kirby put down the window, leaned out, and pressed the button on the speaker box. Instantly a man's voice said, 'Yes. Can I help?'

'Detective Inspector Reid and Detective Sergeant Kirby to see Lord Peter Ripton!'

The security camera silently moved, looking down at the car. No sound came from the speaker box. Nothing happened. Kirby was about to press the button again when both gates swung slowly open.

Kirby inched the car slowly over the cattle grid. Ahead, a ribbon of black tarmac protected on either side by a white-painted post and rail fencing and spaced evenly along the fence, an avenue of chestnut trees. Beyond that, open grassland and small groves of trees. As they drove towards the house, they saw deer grazing on the new spring grass. One watched them from the trees. It paused only a second, then bounded away, its white tail erect.

The road leading to Ripton Hall ended in a circular driveway. On a grassed area in front, surrounded by a bed of roses, was a pond. In it was an ornate fountain topped with the statue of a crying angel, its wings outstretched.

'Quite a place?' Kirby said as she got out of the car.

'Impressive. Downton Abbey all over again?' said Reid, turning a full circle, taking it all in.

Directly in front of them was a series of wide stone steps leading to the front door of the house. From it, a man emerged. He walked forward and leaned over the waist-high balustrade. He stood, hesitant, looking down as if unsure whether to walk down and greet them or wait for them to come to him. Finally, after a few moments, he descended. As he cleared the last step, Reid and Kirby walked over to where he stood.

'Lord Peter Ripton? I'm Detective Inspector Mike Reid, Kingsport CID.' Reid showed his ID. 'This is my colleague, Detective Sergeant Marcia Kirby.'

He nodded to them.' Inspector, sergeant. This is unexpected. What can I do for you? I hope you are not selling tickets to the Police Charity Ball. Because, if you are, the Chief Constable beat you to it. I've already got them?'

Reid noted the reference, name-dropping! Was that casual mention of the Chief Constable being an acquaintance done to impress or intimidate, Reid thought?

'No, sir. We're not here about that.'

'Well, inspector. How can I help you?'

'We are here inquiring about a man found dead in the churchyard at Corn Hill last Saturday. His name was Maurice Wilson. '

'Yes, inspector. I read something about it in the newspaper. But I don't see how I can help you!'

A few raindrops hit the ground, causing Lord Peter to gaze skywards. 'Looks like more coming? Another April shower. Shall we adjourn to the summerhouse, inspector?' He pointed. 'It's just around the side. If you'd follow me?'

Reid and Kirby followed in silence. Then, leading the way, Lord Peter took them around the side of the house, past stables, a garage and up the steps into the summerhouse just as the rain started. The front of it was all glass, while the remaining walls were oak-paneled. In each corner stood a full-size figure in a suit of armour. Above them was a sloping glass roof with retractable sun blinds. Kirby pictured herself sitting out here on a warm summer evening, drinking wine and watching the sunset.

'Impressive view,' said Kirby, looking through the glass wall at the rose beds and the parkland beyond.

'Yes. Nice, isn't it? Please, take a seat. Can I get you some refreshments? Tea, coffee?'

Declining the offer, they both sat. The room was plush, the décor lavish. There were three couches, a chaise lounge, two armchairs, and a table. The couch Reid and Kirby sat on told its own story. It was a testimony to the personality of its owner, money, and wealth. The armchairs, chaise lounge and couches were all upholstered in red silk decorated with white and yellow hand-stitched roses. Kirby felt they were pieces to be admired, not sat upon.

'You say you only read about this man?' said Reid, looking over at Lord Ripton, who was sitting cross-legged in a chair opposite. 'But, according to my information, he came here four days before he died. That was last Tuesday afternoon.'

'You mean it was him, Wilson? He was the dead man that came here?'

'Yes, that was him. Maurice Wilson. He assaulted one of your staff. After refusing to leave, the police were called, and uniformed officers had to remove him. Is that correct, your lordship?'

'Yes, that's correct.'

'Can you tell us what it was he came here for?' Kirby asked.

'He wanted to see my father and insisted he talk to him. I told him my father had suffered a stroke, was paralysed, could not speak, and was in a wheelchair. And asked him why he wanted to see him.'

The door opened, and a woman in green scrubs came in, pushing a wheelchair. In it sat the ailing father, a rug over his knees. Seeing them, she said, 'Sorry, I didn't know anyone was here.'

'Give us ten minutes, will you please? Rita, then it's all yours.'

Without another word, she turned the wheelchair around and left.

Ripton turned to Reid. 'That's my father! The nurse brings him here most afternoons. He enjoys sitting here.'

Reid waited for the door to be closed, then asked. 'Did Wilson tell you anything about what he wanted to talk to your father about? Did he tell you his name?'

'No, he didn't. All he kept saying was that he wanted to see him, and I told him it was impossible to speak to him and asked him again what he wanted him for. At that point, he became aggressive, and then Archer came over. He's my manager, head gardener and gamekeeper, all rolled into one. He asked the man to get into his car and leave, but he got more aggressive and pushed Archer to the ground. At that point, I called the police. It was quite clear to me that the man had been drinking.'

'Was your man hurt?' Kirby asked.

'No. Archer was fine.'

'Mr Archer was well in his rights to have Wilson charged with assault,' said Reid.

'The officers here did point that out, but Archer declined to do so.'

'Maria Jankowski. Does that name mean anything to you, sir?' Reid asked

The expression on the aristocrat's faces changed. He looked at his watch. 'No. I'm afraid not. I've never heard that name before; it's unfamiliar to me.' He rose from his seat. 'Now, if you have no more questions, Inspector, I have a crucial board meeting I have to attend in London. I need to be there by five, so if there's nothing else I can help you with, I'll have you shown out?'

'One last question, sir. Where were you last Friday night?' In an irritated voice, he replied, 'Well, I don't think it's any of your business, but if you must know, I spent Friday night at the Parkside Hotel in Mayfair.

'I think we have all we need, sir,' Reid said, looking at Kirby to see if she had questions. 'We can see ourselves out. Thank you for your co-operation.' They both stood and made their way to the door.

Outside, the rain had stopped, and as the pair walked back to their car, Reid saw the garage doors were wide open. Inside two cars were parked. One was an open-top Land Rover, and the other was a red Ferrari sports car. Reid stood admiring the sleek lines of the car when a voice behind him said. 'It has a 478PS 3.0-litre V8 engine and a complete Tulio Inconel LM Competition exhaust system.'

Reid turned to see a tall, well-built, elderly man standing a few yards away. He was wearing bib and brace overalls and, on his head, an outsize tartan cloth cap. Over his shoulder was a garden spade. He held it like a soldier on guard. Archer! Reid thought? It has to be!

'You don't need to understand how engines work to get a sense of how wild this car is–even when it's standing still, it's self-evident.' Archer said.
Reid had no argument about that.

'You must be the police?' He pronounced it *polis*. There was the trace of Somerset in the voice. 'Rita. Rita Mercer, the nurse, said she saw you in the summerhouse.'

'I take it you must be Mr Archer?' Kirby said. 'I'm Detective Sergeant Kirby, and this is Detective Inspector Reid.

'Gordon Archer. Yes, that's me.'

'Mr Archer, I believe you were here last Thursday and witnessed a disturbance between Lord Peter and a man called Maurice Wilson?' she asked.

'Yes, the fracas. I was here, but I didn't know the chap's name. I read later that he was dead?' Archer said, looking at her. 'The officer, the big intimidating fellow with the curly hair, took him over to his car and took his details, then sent him off with a flea in his ear.'

PC Ambrose thought Reid. He fits that description. 'Has Wilson ever been here before?' Reid asked Archer.

'No, not to my knowledge. He hasn't.'

'Have you worked here long? Mr Archer?' asked Kirby.

'I started here back in nineteen eighty-eight. Thirty-two years ago, long before even young Lord Peter was born.'

'Lord Peter told us he knocked you to the ground? You decided not to press charges, I'm told?' Kirby said. Why was that?'

'A lot of good that would have done me now with him being dead. Anyway, it wasn't me that decided. It was his lordship who told me not to bother. He didn't want any fuss. Said I shouldn't speak to him or the police because he said it wasn't in the public interest. He said we shouldn't have anything to do with Wilson and that if he was to turn up again, call the police straight away. He told that to all the staff!' Archer looked at his watch. 'Four o'clock. It's time I was away!'

'Ah, I see. So, you need to be somewhere?'

'I do. And If I don't turn up for a pint and a game of dominoes at the Red Lion before I go home, they'll send out a search party for me.' He laughed. Archer then walked off. 'Okay, thank you, Mr Archer,'

Kirby looked at Reid. 'Strange? Why would Lord Ripton tell Archer to keep quiet?' said Reid. 'I think his lordship knows more about what Wilson wanted than he's letting on? He's hiding something!'

Another April shower could be seen in the distance.

'Come on, Marcia, let's get to the car before that lot hits us!'

Chapter Sixteen

It was late afternoon when Carter returned to his office after meeting with Commander Watkins. He thought of calling it a day when he was alerted by an audible ping. It was an incoming email. The icon in the tray started flashing. Hoping it was from forensics, he tossed the budget report that Watkins had signed off on into the desk drawer, shut it, and sat down. Carter brought the mail in and clicked on the attachment. The folder contained everything forensics had found at the burial site. It had been photographed in situ and closeup.

Carter set up a slide show and then slowly went through them. When he got to the seventh item, a bracelet, he stopped and leant forward. Clicking on the magnifier icon, Carter enlarged the image and scrutinised it. After a while, he leaned back in his chair. He placed his hands on his head and stared at the screen in disbelief. Could it be? Was it the same one?

He reached for the phone and hastily tapped the lab's phone number. He sat impatiently, drumming his fingers on the desktop, staring at the screen while waiting for someone to answer. It rang and rang. After what seemed an age, it was picked up.

'Yes.' said a voice Carter didn't recognise.

'It's DCI Carter. Is Tim about?'

'No, sorry, inspector, he's still out. What's it about? Can I help you?'

'The remains found at Oxney,' said Carter.

'Ah, yes. Laura's handling that one. Do you want to speak to her?

Hang on. She's here. I'll get her for you.'

'Okay, thanks.' Carter heard muffled words, approaching footsteps, and then the voice of Laura Townsend.

'Chief Inspector Carter, good afternoon! What can I do for you?'
she asked.

'Laura, hi! That tiger eye bracelet. The one from Oxney Wood. Did you find anything with it?'

'Sorry, what did you mean, find anything with it? Such as what?'

'I believe it might have had a small gold charm attached to it. It's a Sango Nigerian charm bracelet.'
There was a long silence. All Carter could hear was her breathing.

'How do you know all this?' she asked.

'I'm sorry, Laura, I can't say too much, not at this stage. I need to check, but I think I might know who it belonged to.'

It was like putting together a jigsaw puzzle. Bits of Carter's memory started falling into place, the picture slowly taking form from that day years ago. The image he saw was of himself standing in the living room of a small cottage a day after it happened. He was taking notes and asking questions.

Carter returned to the present. He thought for a moment, then said to Laura Townsend, 'The Sangos are an ethnic group in Africa. This charm, the one I'm thinking of, was gold and shaped like the map of Nigeria. Sango is one of the Orishas. The Orishas are a deity, a god in the Yoruba culture from Nigeria. Look it up sometime!' He was surprised he remembered the details.

'Yer, thanks, maybe I will.' She sounded uninterested. *'Look, Tim and his team are still out at Oxney. They'll be heading back pretty soon! I'll get them to run the detector over the ground before they go. If it's there, our detector should find it! It's that, or we sift the whole site.'* She paused. *'That could take days and, of course, money. Do you want to sanction it?'*
'Just the detector, but remember, you're looking for something small!'
'If it's there, we'll find it.'

'Okay, Laura, thanks. Let me know how you get on?' He put the phone down and continued staring thoughtfully at the computer screen.

All thoughts of leaving were now forgotten. Carter needed to remember, and he needed the files. Some would be on the system. A lot of the paperwork and the notebooks from the case would be stored where it all started, Canterbury! Reaching for the phone, he thought that tomorrow he'd start the investigation afresh, and this time with him in charge, it was going to be run right.'

Before he could pick up, it buzzed. He recognised the Highland accent of Commander Watkin's secretary. Grace Crane jumped in before Carter had time to speak. *'Detective Chief Inspector! Commander Watkins would like you, Detective Inspector Reid and Detective Sergeant Kirby in her office at nine sharp.'* Before he could reply, the line went dead. He was left holding the handset, hearing only the steady purring sound of the dial tone.

Right, he thought. That didn't sound good.

Chapter Seventeen

Wednesday

The sun had only just appeared over the rooftops of Kingsport when Carter drove past the Corner Cafe. He turned up Kent Street and into the parking area behind the back of Kent Street Police Station. There had been very little traffic on the A2 that morning to hinder his run. He'd left Christine still asleep, and the toast he made, he ate on the way. Carter parked the car in his allotted space, locked it, brushed the crumbs from the front of his trousers, and then headed for the side door. The air was still, not a breath of wind. He touched the keycard on the electronic pad. The door clicked open. He pushed through into the rear of the custody suite. He then made his way across and to the stairs that led to the CID room on the first floor.

From down in the cells came shouts, a woman's voice. She was yelling and screaming. Thinking violence was happening, Carter did an about-turn and raced off down the passage. Turning the corner, Carter was just in time to see Sergeant Gary Higgs, the night shift's custody officer, slam the cell door shut. Across the passage, PC Andy Miller lay on the floor, hands between his legs, his face distorted in pain, and kneeling next to him, PC Jane Little.

'What the hell's going on here? Carter asked Higgs.

'Her in there, sir. She kicked Andy Miller in the balls.'

A face appeared, looking out the food hatch of the cell door. 'And I hope it bloody well hurts. That'll teach you to manhandle a woman.'

Realising the hatch was open, Higgs said, 'If you want to make a complaint, by all means, go ahead.' With that, he slammed it shut. It didn't stop her abuse. From inside the cell came more yelling. She was ranting and raving, kicking and banging on the cell door.

'It's Carol Foreman, the one who tried to rob Stukey's with Upton,' PC Little said. 'At three this morning, a railway worker on his way home called it in after seeing her in the railway yard getting into one of the freight wagons. Looks as if she'd been kipping in it. We found the knife on her, pulled her in, and booked her. When it came time to put her in the cell, she turned aggressive, started punching and kicking, and poor old Andy got on the wrong end of her size eight!'

Carter looked down at the huddled form of Miller. 'C'mon, lad. Let's get you up on your feet and get you looked at.'

Carter and Higgs grabbed Miller under the arms and gently eased him to his feet.

'Ouch, shit, steady, that hurts,' said Miller, screwing up his face.

'Once you get home, get the wife to put on a cold compress and kiss it better,' giggled Jane Little.

With a pained look, Miller said, 'You're lucky you don't have them. If you did, you'd know just what pain was.'

****

Happy to see it working, Carter got a coffee from the vending machine and headed upstairs to the first floor. He turned on the lights and then went to his office. Placing the coffee cup on the desk, he opened the Venetian blinds, letting the morning light fill the room. He sat down, sipped his coffee, and waited while the computer booted up. It didn't take long. First thing in the morning, the system was reasonably fast, but as the day wore on and more people logged on, it got slower. Mail popped up.

The first was from Grace Crane, reminding Carter of the meeting with Watkins at nine. He clicked the delete button. The next was from Canterbury University. Diana Thorp, the anthropology professor. It said that she had sent a sample of DNA over to Tim Bryant last night for matching in the data bank. The email said the remains had been in the ground between twenty-eight and thirty years. It was confirming something Carter already knew. But he needed that DNA to be one hundred per cent sure!

Carter looked up at the clock. He had two hours before he met with Watkins. Finishing his coffee, he tossed the empty cup into the wastebasket. As he did, the phone on his desk rang. He reached over and picked it up.

'Inspector, it's Bryant.'

'Morning Tim! You're at it bright and early. Tell me you've got something?'

'I got no hits on the National Data Base, but I got one on the Missing Persons. It belongs to….'

'Let me guess?' said Carter, interrupting him. 'It belongs to a fourteen-year-old Nigeria girl, Adamma Okoro, reported missing in 1991?'

There was a long silence from Bryant. To Carter, it was a sign he'd got it right. 'You still there, Tim?'

'Shit. That's creepy, Bryant said. 'How the hell did you know that? What are you, some bleeding psychic?'

'No, Tim. It was the bracelet. I remembered it from way back. Talking of which, I take it you didn't find the missing pendant?'

'No, Inspector, we did not. And now, if you don't mind, I'll get some breakfast and leave you to polish your crystal ball. I'll email the full report later!'

Carter muttered, 'Okay', and then hung up.

Carter sat for some time, pondering his next move. First, he needed to make some calls. Then, after that, he needed to refresh his memory. And to do that, he'd have to go over everything: every file, every note.

As soon as he finished making the calls, he went to the computer and opened up the files. Just as he got to the second page, Mike Reid tapped on the glass panel and stuck his head around the side of the door.

Carter beckoned him in. Kirby followed him. 'Ah, Mike, you're in? Ah, and you too, Marcia. Come in.'
As he walked in, Reid said, 'Last night, just as I got home, I got a text from the commander. She wants me in her office at nine. Marcia as well! What the hell is going on, boss?'
Carter looked up. 'Who knows? You're not the only one she wants to see. I've been summoned. Well, it's not the budget, that's for sure, because she signed off on that.' He rose out of his chair. 'C'mon, let's see what this is all about!'

Chapter Eighteen

Grace Crane looked over the top of her glasses as the three entered. Her eyes went mediately to the clock on the wall.

'Your twenty minutes too early!' she said, looking flustered. 'Chief Inspector, your appointment isn't until nine o'clock!'

'Yes, I know it is, Ms Crane,' said Carter. 'I'm sure you've heard of the old saying about the early bird catching the worm? And as we are here, we might as well go in.'

'You can't go in. Commander Watkins is busy.'

'As am I, Ms Crane? My team and I have murders to solve. And time is precious. Time and murder wait for no man.' Reid and Kirby stood back, waiting to see who came out on top. Crane or Carter!

It was Carter. He smiled. 'Please don't get up, Ms Crane; stay where you are. We'll announce ourselves.' Carter went to the commander's door, tapped on it, and walked in. Reid and Kirby followed.

Grace Crane got up from her desk and hurried across the room after them. She poked her head in through the doorway. 'I'm sorry, commander, I couldn't stop them!'

Watkins held out both hands as if warding off something horrible. 'It's okay, Grace. Don't worry. It's okay. You can go. Shut the door, please. Crane apologised once again and backed out, closing the door behind her.

Watkins looked up from her desk. 'I guess you're wondering why I've summoned you here?' She looked slowly from Reid to Kirby, then to Carter. Here, her eyes stayed. 'I received a call yesterday from Chief Constable Bishop. He a very upset. He said he got a call from Lord Peter Ripton complaining that DI Reid and Sergeant Kirby harassed him and his staff! What have you to say about that?' Her gaze drifted back to Reid and Kirby.

Carter looked over at Reid, then said, 'I have not yet had the chance to be fully briefed by Inspector Reid on yesterday's investigation. He and Sergeant Kirby were looking into the death of Maurice Wilson. He was the man found in the graveyard. So, at this moment, I'm afraid I cannot answer that question. All I can say at the moment is that Wilson had been to Ripton Hall asking to talk to Lord Peter's father on an unknown matter, and the request was refused. I understand it escalated and resulted in Wilson being escorted from the estate by uniformed officers.'

Reid stepped forward. 'If I may say so, ma'am. There was no harassment, and it was all very cordial. It was a friendly routine interview! Sergeant Kirby and I were seeking clarification, discovering if Lord Ripton knew or had any association with the dead man!' He turned, looking at Kirby.

'That's correct, ma'am. His lordship even offered us tea!' added Kirby.

'That doesn't sound like harassment to me,' said Carter. Watkins pushed back her chair and stood up. She came around the front of her desk and addressed Carter.

'Lord Ripton is a big donor and patron of several charities, one of which the Chief Constable is a chairperson and one that he is very fond of. So, you can see why he's upset! The Chief Constable has assured Lord Ripton that you will not go there again!'

'Commander,' said Carter. 'I think you know me better than that? Chief Constable Bishop may have given Lord Ripton that assurance, but I can't. I have a murder investigation to run. If there are more questions to ask this man, then so be it. I am not prepared to put up with any outside interference!'

'He's not a suspect, ma'am. He was staying at the Parkside Hotel in Mayfair. I checked it out,' Kirby said.

Watkins looked at them both. 'So. Have you been checking up on him? Okay, Inspector Reid, Sergeant Kirby, that will be all for now. You may go.'

After Reid and Kirby had left and closed the door behind them, Commander Watkins returned to her seat and said to Carter, 'I had a feeling you'd say that. You put me in a hell of a position. You know, Bob. Sometimes you can be too stubborn for your own good. You can be a bit of pain, but remember just who you're going against? Are you prepared to take on that fight?'

'I'm sure if you talk to him nicely, he'll understand?'

'Why do I get the impression I'm wasting my breath? Bob Carter, sometimes you can be a real bastard.' She threw her hands in the air. 'I give up. On your head, be it!'

Carter smiled. 'I knew you'd see it my way.'

'Ok. It's your funeral, Bob! You can go.'

Carter walked over, grabbed the door handle, and pulled it open. Stopping, he turned, looked back and said, 'Those bones found at the Oxney site! You might like to know I've got the DNA back.' He looked at her for a moment in silence, then said. 'They belong to Adamma Okoro! Do you remember her?'

Watkins looked up in surprise. 'My God! Adamma Okoro. Yes. I remember her. She was the Nigerian girl who went missing when we were both working in Canterbury?'

'Yes, it's a match. It's her, Adamma.' Softly, he said. 'I've finally found her! So now I have to tell her parents.'

He walked out, closing the door behind him. He returned to his office, pulled down the blinds and started going through the evidence boxes sent to him from Canterbury.

****

One hour later, Carter entered the incident room carrying the two archive boxes. He set them down on the table next to where Hollingsworth and Richardson stood talking.

'There we go. These are for you.' Carter said. He set them down on the table.

'What are they?' asked Richardson.

'These are all you want to know about the investigation into the disappearance of Adamma Okoro, a young Nigerian girl. Please familiarise yourselves with them. We've got a job on our hands and a lot of work to do on this one.'

Hollingsworth opened the lid of one box and looked inside. He was expecting to see a few sheets of paper but was surprised to see it was nearly half full of files, photos, and scraps of paper.

He looked at Carter. 'All this from a few bones? Forensics have only had them a day. And they got all this from that? I think young master Timothy is playing silly beggars with us?'

'No. It's no joke, Luke. You only have to look at the date on the boxes to see that!'

Richardson twisted one around so she could see. Looking at the date and then at the name, she asked, '1991. Anyway. Who's Adamma Okoro?' she asked.

Carter placed two photos down on the table. One was the skeletal remains taken from the site. The other was of a young, dark-skinned teenage girl. With her was a group of teenagers. One had his arm resting on her shoulder.

'This is Adamma Okoro, aged fourteen. She was Nigerian. Disappeared while walking home after a night out with friends.'

'A cold case? she said, picking up both pictures. 'Shouldn't we be handing this over to the cold case unit?'

Carter took some papers from the opened box and laid them on the table. He flicked through them, occasionally stopping and reading the contents. 'No, Jill. Not this time. This one is all ours, or should I say, mine! No one's taking this one from me.'

'Why us?' asked Hollingsworth.

'I'll explain all that in a moment,' replied Carter. He took more papers from the box. 'These are in a mess. Some files have been digitised, but this lot has just been tossed in. Nothing here is in order. I want them time lined and put in chronological order. Date first! We'll need them for cross-referencing later. I'll see if Inspector McPhee can spare one of his plods to lend a hand!' Walking to the window, he pulled out his phone.

'Blimey. I've never seen the boss this wound up before!!!' Hollingsworth said quietly to Richardson.

Richardson pulled the other box towards her and took off its lid. Inside was a stack of MG11 witness statement forms and notebooks. Some statement forms had been filled out, and others were left blank. She took one out, read through it, and then, without a word, handed it to Hollingsworth. She pointed to the bottom where it said, *Signature witnessed by:* 'Look at the signature!'

It was signed, *Act DC R Carter*. 'Acting Detective Constable Carter?' said Hollingsworth. 'I think that explains my, why us, question.'

Carter came back over to the table. 'Inspector McPhee said he can spare PC Little. He said she's an excellent researcher and correlator, so make the most of her!'

'Sir,' said Hollingsworth. 'This signature. Is this yours?' He handed Carter the statement.

Carter reached out, took it from his outstretched hand, and said, 'Yes, lad, that's mine. After leaving the Police Training Centre at Ashford, I went to Canterbury. One year out as a PC, I was seconded to help CID, and the first job my DCI gave me was to look for a missing girl. The family had only been in the country for two years. She lived with her parents in a cottage at Leegate Bottom. Ironically, that's only a few miles from Oxney Woods, where she was found! Her father was a draftsman for the Town Planning dept, and her mother was a dental receptionist in Canterbury. On Saturday, the eighteenth of May, she met with friends in Canterbury. They went to the Marlowe Theatre to see a show called Charley's Aunt. She loved the theatre and acting. It was her ambition, one day, to be an actress. Afterwards, she and her friends had fish and chips, and she caught the last train home. She was seen to get off the nine-forty-four at Snowdon by three other passengers. Their statements said they followed her up the steps, onto the road and over the bridge. At that point, the three turned right, leaving her to continue towards the village of Woolage. It was where she lived, and that was the last anyone saw of her!' He pointed at the two boxes. 'It's all here. Please read it. Memorise it.'

Hollingsworth stared at Carter. 'And you still remember all those details after all this time?'

'Not all, Luke, just some,' replied Carter. 'This one is special to me.'

Carter moved to the other side of the table and sat down. 'To understand, I'll have to tell you why I'm taking this on. It's because an injustice was done! The only setback in finding her was my boss, DI Rigby. He took early retirement. He went two months after I joined CID. I had my suspicions at the time that something was not right about him, but being the new boy, you kept your mouth shut and got on with it. Even his team was afraid to question his approach. I often wondered if they knew, or come to that, if they even cared. He never took the search for her seriously. Some leads weren't followed up, and interviews were not done. It was a total mess. A cockup from start to finish. Her parents went through hell. Their calls to Rigby went unanswered, and they were often left talking to uniformed PC who knew bugger all. It wasn't until after I came here a few years later that I discovered the truth. Rigby was a card-carrying bigot, a white supremacist. He'd have quite a few things to answer for if he were here today.' Angrily he said, 'That bastard didn't want her found. He never gave a shit about her or the parents. In those days, the new boys got all the shit jobs, filing, making tea, and running errands. I was lucky! I was with the investigation team. Even as a novice, I could see the investigation was going nowhere, and things that should have been investigated were ignored.

She was just listed as a missing person. Well, now she's been found, things will be different. If her killer is still out there, I want him found. I want answers. I owe it to her and the parents!'

'Sir, without stating the obvious, some witnesses may longer be alive,' said Hollingsworth. 'Maybe even the killer himself?'

'Yes, Luke. I realise that. It's up to us to find that out. I didn't expect this to be an easy one to crack! Not after all this time.'

Richardson posed the question. 'Were there any suspects?' she asked.

'Yes, Jill,' answered Carter. 'Quite a few. To earn a bit of pocket money, Adamma would sometimes go strawberry picking. The farm was only a few miles up the road from her, just a short walk, close to the railway station. Backpackers used to camp out in huts and tents during the season. That farm was our starting point because Adamma would have had to have gone past it on her way home from the station, and she would have known some of those pickers. Some pickers were interviewed. Six we couldn't find. One of them could have killed her!'

Carter went over to the window and looked down into the car park. 'Now I have to break the news to the parents. At least they'll have closure and be able to bury their daughter with dignity.' He turned to face Richardson. 'Jill, if you're up to it, I'd like you to come along?'

'Yes, I'll happily come.' Richardson saw the hurt written on his face. 'You've got nothing to reproach yourself about, boss. You did what you had to do and carried out the orders you were given; what happened back then was not down to you!'

Chapter Nineteen

Bill Turner forked the last piece of apple pie into his mouth and then pushed the bowl away. He drained the orange juice from his glass, got up from the table and, picking up the tray with its dishes and cutlery, walked over to the mobile trolley and set it down. Then, leaving the constant buzz of conversation behind him, Turner headed towards the door. He walked through the swing doors, along the passageway, and, climbing the stairs, walked into the work area a few moments later.

He sat in front of the computer and wriggled the mouse to wake it up. Earlier that morning, the enquiries he'd sent to the Immigration Department and Border Force were in the inbox. Turner opened them, reading and making notes as he went. Finally, after checking a few websites, he had all he wanted. He got up, walked to DI Reid's office, and tapped on the door. Reid was on the phone but beckoned him in.

Turner walked over to Reid's desk and, as he put the phone down, **he said.** 'I got that Maria **Jankowski** information you asked for!' **he said.**

'Good. That was quick work! I didn't think it would be that easy?'

'Guess I caught them on a good day?'

'Okay. So, what have you come up with?'

Turner looked down at the notepad he was holding. 'Maria Jankowski. She's Polish and left Gdansk in 1985. Her parents died in 1976 during a worker's protest. Both were shot by police. At age 15, they classed her as an orphaned special refugee and brought her to the UK to live with her only relative, an aunt outside Kingsport. The information I have is that the aunt died two years after Maria arrived. There's still a big Polish community living over in the Moreton Estate. They're all relatives of refugees that came here after the second world war. They've got a social club, and I have a few contacts. Do you want me to see what I can find out? There's a good chance someone there may even know where she's buried. I could also check for employment records as well?'

'For the moment, Bill, let's keep that on the back burner. I've been thinking. Go to the Sisters of St Paul at Ivy Hatch and see what you can find. I've got a theory, and If I'm right, it could help clear a few things up!'

****

Seeing the signboard pointing to the B2046, Carter turned off the A2, then toward the roundabout, through it and headed toward Snowdon. Shortly after, he reached the bridge spanning the railway line. He slowed and drove across. Below was the unmanned railway station. Once over, he stopped the car under some trees, got out, and walked back to the bridge.

'What are we doing?' Richardson asked, getting out and following him. 'Sightseeing?'

'Yes, Jill. I am. The last time I was here was nearly thirty years ago. I'm doing the same thing now as I did back then. I'm retracing her last steps.'

Carter stopped in the middle of the bridge. Leaning over the low wall, he looked down at the station below. As he stood watching, a train came in on the down-line platform and screeched to a halt. It waited. Nobody got off, and nobody got on. Then, with a short blast on the horn, the train was off again, gathering speed as it went. Standing on the bridge, Carter tried to conjure up a picture of the fourteen-year-old as she walked the length of the platform, up the three flights of stairs, and onto the road. After a few minutes, he turned away. 'Okay, Jill. Let's get back to the car!'

Once in the car, he drove on a little further, did a three-point turn in the entrance to the old colliery, drove back over the bridge, and headed towards the village of Woolage. He'd only gone about half a mile when he pulled off to the side, stooped the car and put down the window. He pointed to the flock of sheep in the field.

'I remember. This was once part of a strawberry farm!' said Carter. 'And over there, under those trees, three huts where pickers could stay.'

He drove on a few hundred yards further on, then stopped again. On the road verge was a signpost, its finger pointing out a public footpath, a right-of-way across the field. Carter switched off the engine, got out and looked around, familiarizing himself. On the far side of the field stood Oxney Wood. Kirby came up behind him.

'I don't think Adamma Okoro was killed elsewhere, moved, and buried in the woods. Why would you take the body all that way? Why not just bury her in this field? The more I think about it, the more convinced I am that she was taking this shortcut across the field and through the woods to get home. That was somewhere in those wood she met the murderer! She knew this area well. Keeping on the road and going through the village is the longest way home.'

'You think the killer may have known that and was waiting for her?' Richardson asked.

'No, Jill. I think whoever killed her saw her and followed!'

'Maybe she even knew the killer, and he walked along with her?'

'Yes,' it's possible,' agreed Carter. 'There is that possibility. If an initial search of those woods had been carried out in the first place, we wouldn't need to be here!' Carter sighed. 'C'mon. We still have a job to do. We're nearly there, just a little further on.' They walked back to the car.

Chapter Twenty

Carter drove through the village of Woolage and, a few minutes later, brought the car to a halt outside the cottage where Adamma Okoro's parents lived. Before leaving Kingsport, Carter checked to see if, after thirty years, the couple was still there. Thirty years on, they were!

'Nice little place?' said Jill Richardson, getting out of the car and checking out the surroundings. 'A bit out of the way, but nice all the same. Too far from the nightlife for my liking.'

Carter shut the car door and stood on the pavement looking at the white-fronted cottage. It was just as he remembered. Nothing much had changed. The only thing he remembered not being there on his first visit was the garage and the driveway. Both were new add-ons. The field surrounding the property had changed. The last time he was here, it was carrots, a vast sea of them. Now a new moneymaker had taken their place. Cherries.'

He turned to Richardson. 'Do you know what the name Adamma means?' he asked.

'No. It sounds more like a boy's name to me,' said Richardson, closing her door.

'No, it's a girl's name. It's Nigerian for a beautiful girl.' A daughter never to return, he thought.

A privet hedge, shoulder height, ran along the road frontage of the cottage. In the centre sat a white wrought-iron gate. Its hinge squeaked as Carter pushed it open. On the lawn, a dark-skinned man was busy raking leaves. Hearing the squeak of the gate, the man stopped and looked up. He took a handkerchief from his pocket and wiped his brow. Carter and Richardson walked down the path towards him.

'Mr Okoro?' He held out his identity wallet for the man to see. Richardson held out hers. 'I'm Detective Chief Inspector Bob Carter, and this is Detective Constable Jill Richardson. I wonder if we might have a word, please?'

Replacing the handkerchief, he said, 'Yes, certainly. Please, call me Samuel. Let's go to the house, shall we? It will be a bit more comfortable there. I'll get the wife. Oni, to make us some tea.' Samuel Okoro dropped the rake onto the pile of leaves he'd gathered. 'Please follow me.'

Mr Okoro led them down the path and into the house. He ushered them into the sitting room, seated them, and said, 'I'll just let the wife know you're here. She's in the kitchen. Excuse me. I won't be a moment!' He turned and left. Sitting in the armchair next to Carters, Richardson said quietly, 'Do you think he knows why we're here?'

'I thought maybe he recognised my name?' said Carter. 'Obviously not!'

A few moments later, Okoro appeared in the doorway. 'Tea is on its way. I must admit that when they said they'd send someone around, I didn't expect them to send two detectives, especially a Chief Inspector. I didn't think they'd send anybody. I only called last night! I'm impressed. Those hoodlums need locking up and their bikes confiscated.'

'I think we may be at cross purposes here, Mr Okoro,' said Carter. 'We're here on an entirely different matter.'

'So, you're not here about the bikers using the road outside my house as a racetrack?'

'No,' said Carter, shaking his head. 'We are here on a different matter entirely.'

The man looked crestfallen. He flopped down on the couch opposite. 'Well, I thought it was too good to be true!' He suddenly became alert. With eyes staring, he leant forward. 'Then why are you here?' he asked.
Before Carter could answer, Samuel Okoro's wife, Oni, came in carrying a tray. She set it down on the coffee table in front of them.

'Who are these people, Samuel?' she asked, unsure.

'I just told you out in the kitchen who they were, my dear. These people are from the police! Sit down. I'll pour the tea.' She sat down on the couch beside him. Samuel Okoro poured one for Carter and handed it to him. 'A biscuit?' he asked. Carter declined. Okoro set about pouring out another cup.

'Mr Okoro, I don't know if you remember me, but I was part of the original investigation team looking into your daughter's disappearance.'

At the mention of her name, Samuel Okoro looked up. The tea he was pouring overflowed into the saucer. He slowly put the teapot onto the tray, his hands trembling slightly.

'Adamma is in school in Canterbury, but she'll be back later!' said his wife. 'You're like her; she's a nice girl!' Carter and Richardson looked at Oni, then at Samuel Okoro.

'I'm afraid there's no hiding it, Inspector. My wife is suffering from dementia!' He patted her on the knee. 'Some days, she remembers. On others, well, she's not so good!'

'I'm sorry to hear that,' said Richardson.

Carter placed his cup down on the coffee table. 'Mr Okoro, I have come here to tell you we've found some remains not very far from here. We are ninety-nine per cent sure that it's those of Adamma.' He paused, allowing Samuel Okoro to absorb the news. 'They were discovered on Monday, up in Oxney Wood.'

Okoro slowly placed one hand across his mouth. From behind it came a muffled cry. Reaching out, he grabbed his wife's hand.

'Are you sure it's her?'

'We are. But to be one hundred per cent sure, we'd like a sample from you for a DNA test.'

'How did she die?'

'There was a depressed fracture to the side of the skull.'

'But I don't understand. Who could have done such a thing? You said she ran away, left home?'

'Me!!!' answered Carter, surprised.

'Yes, you, the police. The one who came a few days after Adamma's disappearance, that inspector, Rigby? He said she'd run away and said he had evidence!'

'What evidence?' Carter asked, looking surprised.

Okoro looked into the face of his wife. It was expressionless. No love, hate, or recognition showed on it. It was like looking at a blank canvas. It was like she did not hear any of their conversations. He turned back to Carter.

'I'm sorry, inspector, I'm confused. He said she was seen getting on the train to London! I asked him. Why would she leave and take nothing with her?'

'No, Samuel! I can tell you that your daughter never got on any train to London because Adamma was killed while walking home from the train station,' said Carter.

Okoro shook his head. 'Then how come that other police officer said that to me?' There was a long pause, then he said, 'My God!!!

'That said, we have re-opened the case, and I will do all I can to correct the wrong done to you and your wife! I intend to see that there is an open inquiry into the mismanagement of that investigation.'

'Is Kevin coming to dinner tonight?' Oni asked her husband.

Okoro looked at her. There was sadness in his eyes. Okoro looked defeated. He sighed. 'No dear. He's gone. That was a long time ago. He won't be back.'

'Your son?' Carter asked.

'No. A friend of Adamma's, Kevin Peterson.'
Looking his age and with tears in his eyes, he said, 'Kevin's father owned the strawberry farm. Adamma sometimes went there on weekends to earn a bit of pocket money. Kevin was sweet on Adamma. He was four years older than her, and she was only a schoolgirl. I was not entirely happy with that at all. They went out a few times. After her disappearance, he came around a few times asking if the was any news, but after about a week, he stopped coming. I think now he's married with a family.' He sat back, hands on his knees. 'All this talk has stirred up old memories. If you don't mind, Inspector, my wife needs to rest, and I need time to think.'

Carter nodded, then rose to his feet. 'Yes, certainly. I'll keep you fully informed. In a day or two, we should be able to return her and her personal effects!'

'What affects?' Okoro asked.

'Her bracelet was found at the site,' said Carter. He took out his phone and showed him the picture.

'I had truly forgotten about those. Adamma loved them and wore them always. She never left home without them. Apart from the one with the charm, they were a matching pair!'

'So Adamma would have been wearing both when she disappeared?'

'Chief Inspector. As I told you. She hardly ever took them off!'

'Just one more thing before we go. This ring was found at the site.' He scrolled to the next picture. 'Do you recognise it? Did this belong to your daughter?'

'No,' Okoro answered. 'Definitely not. She never wore rings. She was never ever into those things.'

****

Sitting in the car minutes later, Carter found it hard to control his anger. He slammed his hand down on the steering wheel again and again and again. It was so violent and unexpected that it made Richardson flinch. Having never seen Carter like this, she stared at him. His anger surprised her.

Carter sat there. All he felt was anger. He took a minute to compose himself, then pressed the button, sending the window down.

'Can you believe that bastard? That makes me feel sick to my stomach. Rigby went back and told them she'd run away. Jesus Christ! I bet when he left this house, he had a grin on his face from ear to ear.' Then, staring back at the house, he said, 'Jill, I need to get someone to look at Rigby's past cases. They'll need to look into any involving non-Caucasians. I don't think this is the first time he's done this?'

'You think he was that racist he'd do such a thing?' Richardson asked.

He turned to her, saying, 'Jill. I don't think. I know! You've just witnessed it with your own eyes. What would you say?'

Carter was about to start the car when his phone buzzed. On the screen was the word *Watkins*. Carter leant back in the seat. 'Commander!' A noise! Carter checked the rearview mirror. A tractor with a trailer full of steaming manure came up behind, the driver giving him a friendly wave as he passed. Carter sniffed. Not the best of smells. He put the window back up.

'What the hell was that noise?' Watkins asked.

'A tractor.'

'What are you up to? Where are you?' 'I've just had to tell Samuel Okoro we've found his daughter!'

After a brief silence, she asked, *'How did they take it?'*

'Considering she was murdered and was told by the senior investigating officer she'd run away. I think he took it remarkably well.'

'Run away! What do you mean, run away? Bob, what the hell are you on about? What is it? Is there a problem?'

He thought about telling her, then said, 'I'll explain when I get back.'

'Okay, fine. I'm calling because DC Lynch has requested he return to work. I've spoken to him and the police doctor. DC Lynch doesn't want trauma counselling, and the doc is happy to sign him off, but he comes back on light duties!'

He looked out of the window over at the cottage. 'Fine by me. There's plenty for Dave to do!'

'Okay, I'll see you when you get back?'

Richardson looked over at Carter. 'So, Dave is coming back to work, is he?'

Carter laughed. 'Yep, Monday. It sounds like Maggie has got him doing all those odd jobs around the house she's always on about?'

'Where to now?' Richardson asked.

'Back to the nick, then over to the Bear for a quick one and then call it a day! Tomorrow will be a busy one.'

Chapter Twenty-One

Thursday

Bill Turner walked up to the strapped iron door, reached up, and tugged on the bell pull. From somewhere behind the high granite wall came the clanging of the bell. He stood waiting, hands in his pockets. He'd found Saint Paul's Convent near the small village of Ivy Hatch, six miles outside of Tonbridge. Twice he's had to ask villagers for directions. Reached only by a track, it sat close to a small artificial lake surrounded by trees. It was a minute or two before the bell was answered. Then, finally, a viewing panel in the door slid open. Behind it, peering at him, was a nun, her face wrinkled with age. The wrinkles were so pronounced that Turner found it hard to tell what she must have looked like as a young woman. She looked like a party balloon, almost bereft of its helium, sagged and deflated.

'Yes, can I help you?' she asked.

'I'm here to see the Mother Superior. I called yesterday. My name's Turner, Detective Constable Turner. I'm from Kingsport CID. She is expecting me!'

The hatch slid shut, followed by the sound of a bolt being drawn. A few seconds later, the heavy door swung open. He walked in. 'Thank you, sister.' The old nun pushed it shut.

Turner looked around. He found himself in a Roman-type courtyard. And in the middle, a vegetable garden was being tended by two nuns. A covered walkway surrounded the whole courtyard.

'I'm Sister Monica! The Mother Superior is attending prayer at the moment. She shouldn't be too long! If you'd like to follow me, I will take you to her office, and you can wait for her there.'

As they walked, Turner could not help but notice her bad limp. Then, without turning her head, she sensed his question.

'Polio,' she said. 'The curse of childhood. It was God's will.'

Saying no more, she led Turner across the courtyard and along the walkway. At the far end, he was taken through a door. From there, he followed Sister Monica along a passage. On either side were doors, some open. Turner glanced inside as he passed. He saw a wardrobe, a shelf, and a plain iron-framed bed with a crucifix fixed to the wall above it. The others he looked in were all the same, basic. They were cells, bedrooms without windows. They continued on and up a flight of stairs. At the top, a nun came walking along the passage towards them. 'Here comes Mother Superior now.'

As she drew near, Sister Monica said. 'Mother Superior, a police officer is here to see you!'

'Ah, yes. You must be Detective Turner? Welcome to our convent. I hope you found us without too much trouble. As you know, doubt found out, we are a bit out of the way here?'

'The villagers were very helpful,' Turner replied. 'They pointed me in the right direction.'

The Mother Superior turned, saying to the other nun. 'Thank you, Sister Monica. Would you mind bringing tea along to the library, please?' Sister Monica turned and limped away, back along the passage.

'So, you said over the phone that you wanted to examine some of our records. What is it you are looking for?'

'Yes. It is. I'm hoping you can help with an investigation we're conducting. We're looking for any information regarding a Polish girl called Maria Jankowski. We believe she may have been here at one time?'

'I'm afraid I don't recall the name. Not during my time here, anyway. Sister Agnes is the one to help you. She's our librarian and archivist. Come, she's just down the hall.'

Turner followed the Mother Superior down the hall and into the library. Inside were rows of bookshelves, floor to ceiling, crammed full of manuscripts and leather-bound books. The place was filled with the unmistakable smell of musty old books, stale and damp. Turner's eyes darted around, then over to where a nun sat at a desk. In front of her was a computer screen. Turner guessed the nun to be in her eighties. She stopped and took off her glasses as he and the Mother Superior approached.

After being introduced to Sister Agnes, Turner explained why and what he'd come for. He finished by saying. 'And that is all the deceased had written on the paper, the address of this convent!'

'Maria Jankowski, you say. She, too, is deceased?' Turner nodded. 'If she worked here as a helper or a patient in our hospital, there'd be a record here!' She gave out a laugh. 'Goodie, goodie. Time for a bit of detective work!' Sister Agnes put on her glasses, pulled the keyboard closer, and started typing.

'Sister Agnes is our computer guru. She also runs our Facebook page!'

'The convent on Facebook?' asked a surprised Turner.

'We need to keep up with the times. We can spread the word of God to those outside these walls!'

Turning to the Mother Superior, Turner said, 'Just out of curiosity, has this man ever been here?' He handed her Wilson's photo. She looked at it, then handed it back, shaking her head.

'No, sorry, I'm sure. I can say that because we don't have many visitors. I would have seen him if he had!'

'You're in luck, constable. Here she is,' said Sister Agnes in a triumphant voice.

'You've found her?' said Turner. 'She was here?'

'Yes. Maria Jankowski! She was here in December 1988. In the maternity ward. That was ten years before I came here!'

'It's no wonder I can't recall the name. That's thirty-two years ago! We've had many through our doors over the years. I was only a novice at Saint Cuthbert's College in those days,' said Mother Superior. 'Mother Mary Grace was here then. God rest her soul!'

'Was Maria working here?' asked Turner.

Sister Agnes turned the computer screen toward him. 'No. She was having a baby.'

Turner stared at the screen. 'Having a baby! Are there any other details? The baby, the father?'

'There is a reference number here. I'll need to get those from the files. They haven't been computerised yet. I think I know where I can lay my hands on them. I won't be a moment.' The sister rose from her desk and disappeared into the rows of bookshelves.

The clinking of china disturbed the silence. Sister Monica came in, pushing a tea trolley.

It was the Mother Superior who spoke. 'Ah! Tea has arrived. Thank you, Sister Monica, and, I see, you've brought biscuits. How lovely! You don't have to stay. We can see to it ourselves!'.

'Thank you, Mother,' she said as she turned away. 'I'll pop back for the trolley later?'

Sister Agnes returned a few minutes later, carrying a storage box. She dumped the box down on the desk. After removing the lid, she said. 'Hopefully, it should be here among this lot.' She started sorting through it. Taking the files one by one, she placed them on the desk.

'Ah! Here we are, Maria Jankowski!' Sister Agnes opened up the folder and read from the document. 'Seventeen years old, single. Catholic. She was born on the fourth of March 1970. The address she gave was one in Kingsport, next of kin, Katrina Pabciak, both at the same address. Maria was here from the seventh to the fourteenth. She had a boy. It says he was in our orphanage for five months before being adopted. There's no record of the father's name.'

'Un-married. Maybe she was just one of those poor unfortunate girls who fell by the wayside?' suggested Mother Superior. 'From the records, we know quite a few in our hospital back in those days. Unfortunately, it was closed the following year because our funding was removed. We struggled with the orphanage until 1994. Then that had to be closed.'

'On the birth certificate. What's the baby's and father's name?' asked Turner.

It was the Mother Superior who answered his question. 'The birth certificate we don't have because we had a fire in that part of the library. Those, along with many other records, were destroyed, including priceless parchments, some dating back to the sixteenth century. Some of our remaining records were sent to another convent for safekeeping while we renovated. We only recently started getting them all back. Some never returned.' She pointed to three boxes stacked in the corner. 'I got those back last week. They'll have to be sorted and catalogued. Still, if you want to, you can get a copy of the birth certificate from the General Register Office. 'I can tell you the baby's name, though. That's easy.' Sister Agnes said, looking at one document. The baby's name was given to him by his birth mother. He was called Maurice. Maurice Jankowski!'

Sister Agnes handed the document to Turner. He read it, thinking. So, now we know who he was looking for. It was your mother! Then, turning to the Mother Superior, he said, 'Can I get a copy of this?'

'Certainly, you can. Sister Agnes will see to it for you.'

'Does it say who adopted him? I'd also like a copy of that certificate, please, if I may?' asked Turner.

'Do we have them?' the Mother Superior asked Sister Agnes. 'I do recall losing some in that fire?'

'Yes, we lost some in the fire, mother. They were not kept separate, so it should be here in this file with all the other stuff!' Taking her time, she searched through the rest of the documents. 'You're in luck, constable. Here we are. This is it!' said Sister Agnes, opening an envelope. She took the certificate out. 'A couple living in Brighton adopted him. Arnold and Christine Wilson. I'll make you a copy!'

Well! Maurice Jankowski to Maurice Wilson. That clears up
one thing, through Turner
Inside the envelope, Sister Agnes took out a single sheet of
paper. She carefully unfolded it and then read it.

'It also seems the baby had a secret benefactor! This is a
letter from a firm of London solicitors, Banyon and Croft. It
says that until his adoption, the convent will receive a
donation. Once a month, it will receive the sum of two
hundred pounds to go towards the baby's care and well-
being.'
Both nuns looked at one another.

'Does it say who that generous benefactor was, sister?'
asked Turner.

'No,' the nun replied. 'I suppose you'll need a copy of this
as well?'

'Oh, yes!!!' replied Turner.

Chapter Twenty-Two

Carter walked into the Incident Room, shutting the door behind him. PC Jane Little looked up as he entered. Carter came over and looked at what was on the table.

'How are you getting on, Luke?' Carter asked. Hollingsworth pointed to the folders. 'We're about done. PC Little and I have got most of them time lined and filed chronologically. There's also stuff on the system, but I didn't know if you wanted a hard copy, so I left them?'

'No, that's fine. Leave the files there. Yesterday I found out that when Adamma went missing, she was wearing another bracelet identical to the one found at the site. There's only one on file, and the other one has gone missing. The murder site has again been checked, and Tim assures me it's not there. So it's my guess whoever killed her took it! Did you come across a statement given by Kevin Peterson?'
Hollingsworth shook his head. 'No, nothing from what I saw.' He looked over at Jane Little.

'Did you come across that name, Jane?'

'No, not a Kevin, but there's a statement here by a Martin Peterson!' she said. Then, going to the end of the table, she found the folder and opened it. 'Here it is.'

Carter took it from her and ran his eyes over it. 'This is the farmer, the owner of the strawberry farm at the time! And you sure there's no statement from Kevin?'

'All the statements are here in this folder,' said Little, holding it out. 'Definitely, there is no Kevin and none on the system.'

'Right. Why was Kevin not spoken to?' said Carter. 'That investigation had too many holes in it. It's time we plugged them up! Luke, I want a full background check on this Kevin Peterson. Adamma and he went out a few times, and, according to her father, he was sweet on her. He was eighteen, so that makes him, what, forty-nine? He's married.'

Carter walked to the other side of the table. 'Yesterday, Jill and I passed the Peterson Farm on our way to the parents. It's my guess he may have taken it over from his father! I think he warrants a visit. Also, we need to track down the six who weren't interviewed.'

'Tax records from the farm may help. Then again. They may pay them off the books to avoid tax and paperwork!' said Hollingsworth. 'If that's the case, we've got no chance of finding them!'

'Just do your best, Luke,' said Carter as he headed for the door. He hesitated, stopped, turned and said, 'PC Little, Inspector McPhee, informs me you're an excellent researcher?' Before she could answer, Carter said. 'I've got just the job for you! Come to my office in ten minutes!'

'Sir,' she said. 'Inspector McPhee said he wants me back by mid-day!'

'Don't worry. I'll have a word with the inspector myself. Until then, you can remain here until I tell you otherwise. Is that okay with you?'

'Yes, sir. I'm quite happy to stay.'

'Good!'

Hollingsworth watched him go. Once Carter had left, he said, 'Blimey. He's certainly got a bee in his bonnet about this case!!!'

Twenty minutes later, Jane Little returned from Carter's office with a file containing six names. She found a spare workstation, dropped the folder on the desk, and sat down. Hollingsworth walked over. 'What the hell's the boss got yer doing now?' he asked, looking down at the files.

'These names are case files investigated when DCI Carter was a beat bobby at Canterbury. All this, he told me, is confidential. So, all I know is that I'm looking for anomalies!'

'Anomalies?'

'Yes, Luke. Anomalies. You know? Things that don't look right.'

'Yes. I know what anomalies are.'

'Hey! Be a darling and get me a coffee, will yer, Luke?'

****

'So, what do we know so far about Wilson?' said Reid, looking at the photos and the documents that Turner had taken from the convent and put up on the incident board.

'Adopted at five, he went to live in Brighton. He left school at fifteen, joined the army, and came out a sergeant last year after serving seventeen years. He was medically discharged, suffering from post-traumatic stress disorder. His adoptive parents, Arnold and Christine Wilson, were both dead. As far as I know, he's used no other name. Phone, bank and army records, some of which are classified, are all in the name of Wilson,' said Turner.

'Why would researching his mother lead him to Ripton Hall? I don't understand it. Especially after Lord Ripton denies knowing her.' said Marcia Kirby.

'This mystery man of ours. The one who paid him a visit at White Cliffs. Have we got anything further on him?' Turner asked.

'No, Bill,' replied Reid. 'Nothing. Dave Penrose checked for any home security cameras covering the approach road through the village for the night of the break-in. There was nothing. If only the ones at White Cliffs had been working! The only identifiable prints found in the room were the staff and Wilson. There were others, but they could have come from the previous occupier.'

'What was wrong with the security setup?' Turner asked.

'It was old and was being replaced by a new system. The old one used to play up.'

'Maybe it's worth getting hold of the old system and seeing what's on the recording unit. Yer' never know what we might find?'

'You could have a point there, Bill. Maybe it's worth looking into? Find out the name of that installer. Chase it up, find out if there could be something on it!'

Reid's phone buzzed. He walked off and answered it. A few minutes later, he was back.

'That was Broadbent. Wilson had cancer! It was in the early stages, and Doc said it was not life-threatening.'

'Shit. PTSD and cancer. The poor bugger had nothing going for him, did he?' said Kirby.

Reid turned to the board. 'There's something strange going on there at Ripton Hall, something we're not seeing, and I want to find out what it is?' Reid turned to Kirby. 'The Commander gave us strict instruction to keep clear of Ripton Hall but said nothing about talking to his staff outside the walls? I think Ripton is a man running from shadows?' Reid looked at his watch. 'I think it's time to pay Mr Gordon Archer another call on his home ground, and I know precisely where that is! Who fancies a beer and a game of dominoes in a quaint old country pub?'

'Sorry, boss,' said Turner. 'Count me out. It's the kids' basketball night, and if I miss taking them, Janet will kill me!'

Chapter Twenty-Three

It had just gone five when Reid and Kirby walked into the bar of Red Lion. There were a dozen drinkers in there. Some were sitting nursing glasses of beer at tables, and others were leaning against the bar, chatting. The television above it was showing a game show. Next to that was a notice saying free Wi-Fi for all patrons. The interior reminded Reid of a natural history museum. Moths, and butterflies in frames with mounted stag, badger and fox heads lining the walls, and at each end of the bar was a stuffed squirrel. Reid scanned the faces, looking for Gordon Archer, but he was nowhere to be seen. Reid looked at Kirby, shrugging his shoulders. 'Seems I was wrong!'

Thinking he'd make the most of it, he scanned the menu board behind the bar. Whipped broad-bean mash with flatbreads. Wood-roasted scallops, lobster and chips, followed by a Montgomery Cheddar soufflé. That sounded good. He was about to ask Kirby what she fancied when he heard laughter. Peering around the corner of the bar, he spotted Archer sitting in a small alcove with three other men.

'What will yer have?' asked the barman, walking up to them.

'A pint of yer best, and…' he looked at Kirby.

'Rum and Coke, please,' she replied.

'New?' the barman asked. 'Never seen you in here before?'

'Just passing. We dropped in for a quick one and to see an old acquaintance. Old Gordon over there. Send him one over from me, will yer?' The barman went to get their order.

'You intend to ply him with beer, get him pissed, then get him to confess to a murder?' asked Kirby.

'No, not quite, Marcia. I want to learn more about Ripton Hall's darkest secrets. If anyone knows, it's the staff there, and they're the ones who have their ears to the keyhole!'

'Why do I feel Commander Watkins will come charging through that bloody door any minute now?' Don't worry,

Marcia, we're not being followed. Before coming, I told the boss what I was doing, and he's got our backs. He's just as keen as we are to get this sorted as we are.' The barman returned with their drinks. Reid handed over a ten-pound note, waited for the change, then said, 'Come on, there's a table there. Let's grab it.'

From where Reid sat, he could see the alcove. He watched as the barman went over to the table and delivered Archer his drink. The barman pointed over to where Reid and Kirby were seated. Archer turned his head and looked. Reid smiled and raised his glass in a friendly gesture.

Looking over and recognising Reid, Archer waved. He then said something to his drinking companions, got up, and came over to where Reid and Kirby were sitting.

'Thank you. That's very generous of you. Inspector Reid and Sergeant Kirby, isn't it?' He put his beer down on the table and pulled out a chair.

'Yes, it is,' replied Reid.

'I thought so. I rarely forget a face. Have you been up to the Hall again, have yer?' he said as he sat down.

'No,' Reid said. 'We were out this way on another matter, and as we passed, we thought we'd drop in. Quite a coincidence bumping into you. Is this your local?'

'Aye, it is. Been coming here nigh on thirty-three years. 'He took a big swallow, gulping down half of the glass of beer. He wiped his lips with the back of his hand.

'You would have seen plenty of changes in that time, especially up at the Hall,' said Kirby.

'If you're talking about people, like the staff, and that? Aye, I have. 'He took another swallow, draining the glass. 'The Hall has had its fair share of trials over the years. Lord Peter and his father didn't always see eye to eye. Peter had ideas about new ventures, and his lordship said it would bankrupt them. Anyway, he was given a chance, invested it poorly and lost twelve million.'

'That's a hell of a lot to lose! Bet that didn't go down well?'
Reid said.

'His lordship said Peter would never take over, and
eventually, he would hand the reins over to his brother,
Andrew. Peter was, or should I say, still is, a man who
believes in masters, servants, bosses and workers and never
the twain shall meet if you get my drift. He believes he's a cut
above us, mere mortals. He ain't too bad to me. You take his
dad. Now his lordship was a true gent, old school. He treated
everyone with respect. Andrew and Peter never really got on.
Andrew, like his dad, believed in equality for all. There was a
lot of tension between the two. Andrew had a head for
business, whereas Peter was a spender and risk-taker.'
Marcia Kirby leaned across the table and took Archer's empty
glass. 'Can I get you another, Mr Archer?'

'Thanks, lass. I won't say no, by the way. Call me Gordon.'

'What exactly happened to Andrew, Gordon? Reid asked
curiously.

'That would be some ten years ago. It was a shooting
accident. Andrew was killed while shooting grouse in France.
That was the straw that broke the camel's back when Andrew
was killed. His lordship blamed Peter for taking Andrew to
France and getting him killed. It was a genuine tragedy. As I
understood, Andrew didn't want to go because he was not
into blood sports, but Peter insisted.'
Kirby returned and placed the glass down in front of Archer.

'Here yer go, Gordon!'

'Very nice. Thank you kindly. 'He sucked up the froth and
then took a mouthful.

'What of Lady Ripton?' Reid asked.

'Lady Violet! a lovely lady. No airs and graces about her
ladyship. She took an interest in the village and everybody in
it. She always had time for us workers.'

'What happened to her?' Kirby asked.

'In the end, she just had enough of his gadding around. A
few years after Peter was born, she went off to live in London

and raised him there. He was quite the ladies' man he was. You only have to ask some of the village girls who worked there. They could tell you a few stories, I'm sure! She divorced him later and stayed in London. She moved into a house, one of those they owned in Knightsbridge. Right until she died, she always sent me a Christmas card.'

'Did a Maria Jankowski ever work there?' asked Kirby.

Archer took his cap off and scratched his head. 'With a name like that, I'm sure I'd recognise it, but I can't say I've heard of her. Maybe she was there before my time! You'd have to talk to old Mrs Chester, the old housekeeper. She has a cottage next to the church. If anyone knows, she will! She was there long before me.' He replaced his cap.

'If we need to, we will,' said Reid.

'Why would you want to find out about her?' asked Archer with a puzzled expression.

'The dead man, Maurice Wilson! Maria Jankowski was his mother,' Reid replied. We are just trying to tie up a few loose ends.'

'I noticed when we were up there you had fallow deer? Have you got many?' asked Kirby.

'Twenty-two, not counting the fawns. We're in the fawning season now, and we only have four more doe's to drop their fawns. They are delicate creatures. Fallow deer are easily tamed and are increasing in numbers and distributing slowly throughout the parks and forests of Britain. Did you know there are now more deer in this part of the country today than there were five hundred years ago?'

'Sounds like they keep you pretty busy?' asked Reid.

Archer picked up his glass and took a swallow. 'This is a busy time for us. First, we have to monitor the fawns and protect them from foxes. They try to get in, so we must check the fence daily to ensure the little bleeders are not digging under it. If we see signs of digging, then we put out bait.'

'What do you use?' asked Reid. '1080?'

'No. We don't use that anymore. We have some in the shed, but we use rabbit laced with strychnine. Good lord, is that the time? Archer said, looking up at the clock. 'I really must be going. The wife will wonder where I've got to.' He finished the last of his beer. 'If I see old Mrs Chester, I'll ask her about that woman for you.' He straightened his cap, thanked them for the drinks, shook hands, and headed for the door.

'This jigsaw puzzle still has bits missing, and I think I just know where to find them,' said Reid thoughtfully. 'Ripton Hall!' He watched Archer walk across the bar and out the door.

Chapter Twenty-Four

Friday

The overnight rain had filled every pothole along the track with brown, muddy water. Carter's Ford found them all as it bumped and splashed toward the farmhouse.

'I thought this was supposed to be a strawberry farm?' Hollingsworth said, looking at the horses through the side window.

'Maybe they do both horses and strawberries?' said Carter. He drove through the gate, across the yard, and stopped in front of the farmhouse.

As Hollingsworth got out, he sniffed the air. 'The local community accepts farmyard smells as part of their daily life, but not me,' he said, staring at a giant pile of steaming horse manure. 'Every time I go near one, I come away with half of it on me! Farms and I don't go together!'

As he said that, a black and white Kelpie came out of the barn, barked, and came bounding across the yard towards them, stopped and started sniffing Hollingsworth's trousers. Fearing he was about to pee on him, he pushed the dog away with his foot. As he did, his pants came into contact with the dog's coat. He looked down, cursing. 'Shit. Dog hairs. Bloody farms!'

A man came out of the barn calling the dog's name. The dog turned and ran back over to him. In his mid-forties, the man was dressed in a moth-eaten jumper, dirty jeans, and, on his feet, yellow wellington boots.

'Mr Kevin Peterson?' asked Carter as he approached.

'No. Earnshaw. Roger Earnshaw. The Petersons no longer live here. They left here ten years ago after old Martin died. Old Mrs Peterson is in a home. If you're looking for Kevin, Canterbury is where he is now! I have his address in the house if it's of any help?'

'Yes, thank you. But the sign on your gate said Peterson's Farm?' said Carter.

'I just never bothered changing it. People all know it by that name, so we just left it! Change it, and it just confuses the poor old postman.'

'Are you local?' Carter asked.

'Why do you ask?' he said curiously.

Carter pulled out his ID, introducing himself and Hollingsworth.

'As to your question, yes, Chief Inspector. I was born and bred not two miles up the road from here, in the village. Dad brought this place to set up an agreement for horses.'

'How many do you have?' asked Carter.

'Twenty is what we can take.'

Carter looked around, then focused on the distant Oxney Wood. 'So, no more strawberries?' said Carter.

'No, we got out of them. It was labor-intensive. Had a hard time getting pickers. Turned it all into holding paddocks for horses.' Earnshaw paused, looked from one to the other, and said, 'You must be here about Adamma?'

'Did you know her?' asked Hollingsworth.

'Aye. I went to school with Adamma. We were all led to believe she'd run away. I never knew why she did it. It was all very mysterious. None of us could make any sense of it. But, I don't mind telling you, it came as a bit of a shock when I read they found her in over there the woods,' he said, looking across to the woods where Carter was looking.

'Did you ever come here strawberry picking with Adamma?' asked Carter.

'Aye. We all did. Most of us kids from the village would come here on the weekends to earn pocket money. Mind you. I think we ate more than we picked.' He laughed.

'Did the police ever interview you after she went missing?'

'No. I know I wasn't. I don't think any of us kids were.'

'Can you remember the name of the others here who were with you back then?'

'Maybe, maybe not. That's a long time ago! If I can remember where they are, I got some old photos of us back then, which may jog the old memory. I remember a few Londoners coming down. They'd come for a week or as long as they were needed. They stayed in the hop picker's huts they had here back then. The only thing I can remember about her is her love of acting. She always appeared in our school plays. She loved to act.'

'Did Adamma have any boyfriends?'
Earnshaw thought for a moment before answering. 'Not a steady one, but I know she went out with Kevin once or twice.'

'That'll be Kevin Peterson?' asked Carter.

'Aye, him. Anyway! Come over to the house, and I'll get you that address. Maybe the wife will know where to lay her hands on the photos!'

Earnshaw opened the gate and led them down the path, through the side door and into the kitchen. It was a large kitchen dominated by a sturdy country-style dining table where twelve people could easily sit. Against the wall sat a big Aga stove, sending out its warmth, and next to it, an old-fashioned pine dresser with cups and mugs hanging on hooks. Earnshaw told his wife, Maureen, what Carter and Hollingsworth had come for.

'How about I give these folks a nice cup of tea and a piece of cake while you find the photos?' Earnshaw said.

Maureen Earnshaw walked back into the kitchen five minutes later carrying a box.

'There we go. I told yer she'd know where to find it.'
She put the box on the table and started rifling through the contents.

'Would you like another cup of tea, inspector? What about you, constable, another? Maybe some more cake?' asked Mrs Earnshaw.

'No, I'm fine, thank you, Mrs Earnshaw,' answered Carter.

'I won't say no to another slice of that delicious cake, Mrs Earnshaw,' Hollingsworth answered. 'Your strawberry sponge cake is very moreish.' He handed over his plate.

'I do like a man who enjoys his food. So the secret is to use free-range eggs and fresh-picked strawberries straight from the garden,' she said. She cut him a large slice and handed him back the plate.

'Being a stickler for order, the wife spent the winter evenings sorting the photos into their years, so finding them shouldn't be a problem!' said Roger Earnshaw.

'Sensible idea,' said Carter. 'I might get mine to do the same with ours!'

'Here we go, inspector. He took out a clear plastic sleeve containing several Polaroids. These are all of us, nineteen ninety-one.' He took them out and turned one over. 'And as you can see, all the names are on the back!' He handed them to Carter, saying, 'These bring back memories!'

Carter went through them one by one. Hollingsworth sat next to him, a photo in one hand, a piece of cake in the other. 'Who's this with his arm around Adamma? Is that Kevin Peterson?' Carter asked.
Earnshaw took a pair of glasses from his top pocket, put them on and bent down to look.

'No. That's Liam Crawley.' Earnshaw took a sip of his tea, spooned in some sugar, stirred it, and said, 'He was a sort of creepy kid, lived at the far end of the village. Adamma never got on with him. Neither did some of us come to think of it. Back in those days, a gang of us village kids used to hang around together. Liam included. He never quite fitted in. Did you know his father was an undertaker? Maybe being around dead people had something to do with him being the way he was? Adamma used to call him Creepy Crawley. He hated her for calling him that! Liam took over the family business when his father died. He has a funeral parlour somewhere over Manston way!'

'What does Kevin Peterson do now?' Hollingsworth asked.

'He's got a bookshop in Canterbury, Butcher Lane, just near the Roman Museum!'

'Yes, I know where it is,' replied Carter. 'Funnily enough, only last Sunday, the wife and I were looking at the books in his window!'

Earnshaw picked up a slice of cake, bit into it, then said, 'Kevin was on the parish council for a long time and never did much while there. Then, suddenly, overnight, he turned into a greeny and wanted to save the world. So five or six years back, he campaigned to save Oxney Wood from some developers.'

'Why? What were they going to do with it?' asked Carter.

'Some company wanted to turn it into one of those yuppies weekend retreat and health centres. Do you know the type I mean? Massages and lots of spinach juice! Kevin supposedly spent much of his money, set up a fighting fund, and took them to court. Kevin got a preservation order on it because he said it was a Viking burial site dating back to the days of King Alfred.

Carter rose from the chair. 'Well, we won't keep you any longer. We'll let you get back to work. Is it okay if we take these and have them copied? I'll let you have them back in a couple of days!'

"Aye, by all means,' replied Earnshaw.

A few minutes later, as they were about to drive away, Carter's mobile sounded. Looking at the screen, he saw it was Janice Watkins.

'Are you on speakerphone?'

'No, I'm not. Is there a problem, commander?'

'Nothing that can't be sorted. Are you still with the Okoro family?'

'No. All done. I'm on my way back. I just paid a visit to Patterson's farm.'

'Come and see me when you get back,' she said sternly. Then, before Carter could ask what it was about, she hung up. He slipped the phone back into his inside pocket.

'Okay, Luke, let's get outer here.'

It wasn't until they were heading back along the main road to Kingsport that Hollingsworth voiced his thoughts. He turned to Carter.

'I've been thinking. What if Kevin Peterson knew Adamma's body was buried in the Oxney Wood? What if he heard about the scheduled development, panicked and, fearing she'd be found, sought an injunction against the developers? It makes sense. Don't you think so?

'Putting it into perspective, yes, that sounds plausible. It makes perfect sense,' replied Carter, as he stared out the side window, watching the scenery slide past.

'Another thing? If it was a burial site, how come nothing was found in the sinkhole? You'd think forensics would have found some ancient relic, wouldn't you?'

Carter digested what Hollingsworth had said. 'Yes, Luke. I was thinking along similar lines, and if it's right, that puts Peterson well and truly in the frame. All we have to do is prove it! So, a trip to Canterbury is on the books. It's time we had a little chat with Mr Kevin Peterson!'

Chapter Twenty-Five

PC Jane Little picked up the files and headed out of the incident room. She stood outside in the corridor for a moment, thinking, then hastening to the CID suite; he pushed open the door and marched in.

She looked around. 'Where's the DCI, sarge?' she asked Marcia Kirby. 'Is he back yet?' As she said that, both Carter and Hollingsworth walked into the room. Hollingsworth went over to his desk and sat down.

'Commander Watkins has been looking for you,' Kirby said as Carter approached. ' She told me to pass on a message saying she wanted….'

'To see me the moment I got back,' said Carter, finishing her sentence. 'Yes. I already know, Marcia. She's already been on to me! Thanks.' He turned and looked into Jane Little's face. She stood there looking pleased, like the cat that got the cream.

'Jane! What is it?' he asked.

'Those names you asked me to look into, sir. I've only done six so far and found four anomalies.'

'What's going on? What names?' Kirby said, staring at him. 'What names are these. Is it something we're working on?'

'Not sure. It could be nothing,' Carter said, looking at her. 'I need to look into what PC Little has found first before saying anything.' Carter turned to Little. 'Okay. Let's go to my office! You can tell me there!'

Little followed Carter to his office and closed the door behind her. He told her to sit, saying, 'So, what have you come up with?'

Once seated, she said, 'This one here, it's the one that caught my eye. It's an Indian restaurant broken into and vandalised in 1996,' she said, taking it from the folder and handing the summary across to him.

He spent a few minutes reading it, looked up and said. 'The suspects had been identified on CCTV, but the case never got to court because the video went missing!'

Jane Little nodded. 'Yes, sir. And not only that, but I noticed that three days before the video disappeared, the file on the system was dated and marked for no further action! Another strange thing! Forensics wasn't called in on any of them! These other names, the Asian and Chinese, you gave me. One was a shop owner by the name of Mr Chang Lee. According to the file, Lee was a well-respected community member. He twice accused the police of not following up on his claims about a shoplifter. Mr Lee reported he was verbally abused by the officer-in-charge and stated that there was a racist comment made. It said here there was no report made! Mr Lee was arrested after an anonymous tip-off saying he was selling drugs. After searching his house, they found amphetamines hidden in his garden shed. He swore at the time he was innocent, claiming they were planted on him. He got two years. These others are assaults and robberies, and they were hardly investigated. All had been stamped, no further action within two or three days of the crime being committed.'

Carter took those from her and glanced at them. 'Well, you've done a thorough job of these,' he said. 'Good work, Jane.'

'Thank you, sir. I'll make a start on the others, shall I?'

He didn't answer her.

'Oh, one other thing, sir. I forgot to say. All of them had been signed off by the investigating officer, a DI Rigby.'

Carter nodded. As if I didn't already know, he thought.

'Sir, If I may say so. DI Rigby must have conducted these investigations himself because I could find very little paperwork from other officers on any of those cases, only those of the first responders. So, from what I can see he had done, he initially sent a DC, and then DI Rigby would do the follow-ups?'

'Or, send a wet behind the ears, acting DC,' Carter whispered.

Carter saw himself again, standing in the living room of Okoro's cottage, the first officer on the scene after the teen's disappearance. He thought about how valid Jane Little's words were true. It made sense!

Little questioned him. 'Sir. With him taking over the investigations, does that say he had no trust in his team?'

'No, Jane. Not by any means. It was something else entirely. Hate!'

She looked at him, not understanding.

'It's okay, Jane, thank you. You can go. And again, well done! And just for the time being, keep all this to yourself.'

After Little left, he read through the three remaining reports and started making phone calls. One of them was to Canterbury CID. When he'd finished fifteen minutes later, he picked up the folder and headed for the door. He then made his way through the building to the commander's office. Her secretary, Grace Crane, looked up and smiled as he entered.

'Ah. Chief Inspector Carter. Please go straight in. The commander is expecting you,' she said.

'Thanks, Grace.' He tapped on the door and entered.

'Come in. Sit down, Bob,' Watkins said.

He couldn't help but notice the vase of tulips, daffodils and narcissus. They seemed out of place on her typical clutter-free desk. He sat. As the vase blocked his view, he moved it to one side. A card was attached; on it, Carter saw the name, Tom! He knew straight away where it had come from. It was the Chief Constable himself, Tom Bishop. He was Janice Watkins long-time lover. When Carter was first stationed at Canterbury, Tom Bishop was the Chief Superintendent. It was back then that they had started their affair. What was Bishop's opinion on Rigby? Maybe I should have a word, Carter thought?

'I'm reliably informed that Inspector Reid and Sergeant Kirby have interviewed one of Lord Ripton's staff. Is that correct?' She looked at him from across her desk.

'Yes. Mike and Marcia spoke to him, I believe.'

'You were told explicitly to stay away!'

'Mike told me they met him in a pub. It was a chance meeting, that's all it was, and they chatted. Mike said that he was not in any way coerced and spoke freely. A friendly chat over a pint of beer. They were chatting just like any normal people do over a beer. It was nothing formal. You have my word.'

Watkins gave him one of her. I don't believe your looks.

'He revealed some interesting things about Ripton. Before his brother's death, Lord Peter was told he would not be taking over the business from his father until he learned to control money. Apparently, he lost too many millions in too many poor investments. So the one to take over was the brother, Andrew. Then, low and behold, Andrew gets killed in a hunting accident while in France. So now Lord Peter is next in line for the throne. Is that not suspicious?'

'Are you accusing Lord Peter Ripton, a peer of the realm, of murdering his brother?'

'Yes. I do. I have no proof, but I'm prepared to put my money on it. I've been on to Interpol and spoke with Chief Inspector John-Paul Gerard. He said he would look up the file and give me a copy. According to the French police report, it was death by misadventure. In his interview, Lord Peter states his brother tripped, and the gun went off accidentally. Peter was the nearest to him, and before you ask. No. There were no other witnesses!'

Watkins placed her elbows on the desk and interlaced her finger. She looked across at him, thinking. Then, after a few moments, she said, 'Make sure you have enough evidence before charging around like a bull in a china shop. One wrong move and you could find yourself back on the beat or, worse, out of a job. Are you prepared to risk that? Sticking your neck out like that? Because if you are, I can do nothing to help you. You're on your own, and you know that, don't you? You're in it for the long haul.'

Watkins looked at the folder he had put down on her desk. 'Anything else I should know about?' she asked.

'Yes. These.' He opened up the folder. 'Do you remember DI Rigby from our Canterbury days?'

Watkins nodded. 'Yes. Why?'

Carter told her what had happened to the Okoro family and what Inspector Rigby said about Adamma running away. He then set about telling her what else he had discovered about Rigby.

'If any officers are racist or discriminatory, then I will do absolutely everything I can to make sure they're removed from the force,' said Watkins.

'Since Rigby is no longer on the force, I will suggest that Mr Okoro contact the IOPC and seek compensation by suing the police for emotional distress,' said Carter.

'If what you say is true. Then, yes. Okoro does have good grounds to lodge a complaint with the Independent Office for Police Conduct. Serious complaints and allegations of misconduct like this will also have to be investigated internally. It will have to be investigated by the PS squad. Which means they'll be talking to you as well?'

'Before coming to see you, I spoke with two of Rigby's old team from back then, and they confirmed some of his investigations were shoddy.'

'Okay, well, you contact the Okoros, and I'll call Professional Standards, and they can take it from there.'

'By the way. There's one other thing I want to talk to you about, but it won't happen until after I see her killer sitting in our cells.'

'And what is that?' she asked.

A few minutes later, when he'd finished and left her office, Watkins just sat there staring at the framed photo from her graduation that hung on the wall. It was a surprise, and she envied his decision.

Chapter Twenty-Six

Monday

Carter called for silence, then said, 'First off, let's welcome Dave back into the fold. It's good to have you on the team again, Dave.' There were shouts and applause from those in the room.

'Thanks, boss. Believe you, me. It's good to be back. Maggie was sick and tired of having me under her feet all day. I'm sure she was quite glad to get rid of me.'

'That I can well imagine!' said Marcia Kirby.

'Another day at home, and I think she would have divorced me.'

The door to the incident room opened, and a uniformed PC stuck his head around it. 'Sorry to interrupt, sir,' he said, looking around the room and then at Carter, 'But Inspector Reid's not answering his phone.'

'What is it, constable?' Reid asked.

The constable looked over to where Reid stood. 'There's a lady down in reception asking for you, sir. A Mrs Daphne Webster. She said she'd only speak to you, sir, and said you'd know who she was?'

Shit! Reid thought. He suddenly remembered that he was supposed to have called the guest house on Friday to let her know that Maurice Wilson's room could be released.

'Constable. Take Mrs Webster along to the canteen, will you? Get her a coffee, a tea, or whatever she wants and get her one of those sticky jam doughnuts. That should keep her occupied for a while. Apologise and tell her I'll be there in about ten minutes.'

'Right, sir.' The constable disappeared, closing the door behind him.

Carter looked at Kirby. 'Marcia, I'll run over to Canterbury in the morning. I need to have a chat with Kevin

Peterson.' He turned, saying to Reid, 'Mike! What's happening with this surveillance system from the guest house?'

'Bill was looking into that one.' He looked over in Turner's direction.

'The security firm is on Maple Road over at the industrial park,' said Turner. 'I couldn't get to them sooner because their receptionist said they were on a big installation job up north and wouldn't be back until Sunday night. However, now that they're back, I'll see them today.'

' Okay, Bill. good.' Carter looked over at Dave Lynch! 'You'll need to play catch up. Jill! Bring Dave up to speed, will you please? When you've done that, I want you to dig into the background of Liam Crawley. Crawley is an undertaker over at Manston. He was another one who was never interviewed. He was one of the village lads who hung around with Adamma. They used to call him Creepy Crawley!'

'I can visualise him now,' said Jill Richardson, laughing. 'Tall dressed in black, hunched over and rubbing his hands together like some character out of a Dicken novel.' Remembering the group photo he'd seen at the farm, Hollingsworth said, 'I think you'll find he's short and fat.'

'Okay, He'll need to be spoken to,' said Carter. 'I'll do that. So, that's all there for the moment. Questions?'.... None came. 'Okay then. You've all got your jobs. Let's get at it.'

Reid was the last to leave. He headed along the passage, down the stairs. At the bottom, he turned and walked along the corridor, past the locker room, towards the canteen. Pushing open the door, Reid spotted Daphne Webster sitting at a table in the far corner. Daphne Webster watched over the rim of her cup as he made his way across the floor toward her.

Reid walked past PC Mike Cotton and PC Barry Ambrose, nodding at them as he did. The pair had just come off the night shift and were silently tucking into a hearty breakfast of eggs, bacon, fried bread and toast. What Reid saw on their plates made him envious. That morning, he'd left the house with what Maggie called a healthy breakfast under his belt. Two Weetabix and a dollop of yoghurt was not Reid's idea of a hearty start to the day. To hell with it! He decided he'd grab a bacon sandwich on the way out. The television above the serving counter showed Good Morning Britain, the weekday breakfast programme.

'I must apologise for not getting back to you sooner, Mrs Webster.' Reid said as he neared her table. 'But it's been a hectic week. He pulled a chair out and sat. 'Again, I apologise.' He looked at the half-eaten jam doughnut on her plate. 'I see the constable has been looking after you?'

'Yes, thank you, Inspector Reid. He has. It was most considerate of him. And I quite understand how busy you are, especially after reading the newspaper reports of that poor young girl found buried in the woods. That was shocking.'

Daphne Webster picked up the doughnut and bit into it.' These are very nice. ' She placed the uneaten portion back on the plate, took a paper napkin from the holder and wiped the sugar residue from her fingers.

'We can release the room back to you now, Mrs Webster. We have everything we require.'

'His belongings. Shall I parcel them up and forward them to his relatives? Did you find any?' she asked.

'Sadly, none living,' Reid replied. 'In cases such as these, I suggest you send them to a charity organisation.'

Staring at him, she digested the information for a moment and then said, 'Will he be buried or cremated?' And as an afterthought said, 'Who will pay for it?'

'I can't say what it will be, but in situations with no known surviving relatives or friends, the council will conduct a public health funeral. It's sometimes known as a pauper's funeral.'

'I couldn't bear that poor man buried alone with nobody to mourn him. No one should be. He deserves to be mourned. But, please, can you find out for me when it will take place? I should like to be there to pay my respects.'

Reid nodded. 'Yes. I'll find out for you.'

From across the room came the sound of laughter. Placing their empty plates on the mobile trolley, Reid watched as Cotton and Ambrose, having finished their breakfast, were heading for the door.

Daphne Webster lent over to the chair opposite and picked up her handbag. She opened it.

'This came for Mr Wilson the other day. It was registered. I had to sign for it but didn't know what to do with it, so I thought I'd best bring it here! It may be important?'

She dipped into her bag, pulled out an envelope, and handed it to him. Reid looked at it. It did not show who it had come from or who the sender was. He turned it over to see if there was a return address. Then, he tucked it away in the inside pocket of his jacket.

With that, Daphne Webster pushed back her chair, picked up the last of the doughnut and stood up. 'Waste not, want not,' she said, popping it into her mouth.

Reid smiled. 'I'll see you out,' he said.

Daphne Webster followed Reid along the corridor to the reception area. As the automatic door parted for her, she turned and said, 'Now, don't forget to let me know about the funeral, inspector! Oh, and thank you once again for the refreshments.'

Reid gave her his assurance he would call her. She turned and walked off. He watched as she walked across the car park and onto Kent Street. Once out of sight, Reid turned and walked back to the canteen.

Chapter Twenty-Seven

Bill Turner steered the Ford Mondeo off the main road and into the newer area of the Tizard industrial park. The estate had been named after the Gillingham chemist and inventor Sir Henry Tizard. Before setting out that morning, Turner had to endure the full five-minute lecture on Henry Tizard. Luke Hollingsworth said it was an essay he had to do during his last year at school. Hollingsworth had told Turner that Tizard was famous as the man who conjured up the 'octane rating' that car drivers take for granted these days. He'd also helped develop radar during the Second World War. However, Hollingsworth felt passing on that knowledge had fallen on deaf ears as Turner's only comment, as he headed for the door, was, 'Luke. You're full of shit, you know that!' Turner smiled as he now thought back on it.

Turner stopped by the board displaying the street map. Studying it, he looked for Maple Road. Turner found it tucked away on the far side of the estate, which ran alongside the main Charing Cross, Dover rail line. He drove into the Sure Safe Security Service parking area a few minutes later. It was a clean, white-painted, single-story building set back from the road. A rose between two thorns. To one side of it stood the blue and yellow building of Kingsport Tyre and Brake Services, and on the other, Kingsport Motors, a new car dealership. The premises of Sure Safe were like Fort Knox. It had a high chain-link security fence topped by barbed wire. On each corner sat a security camera.

Turner pulled up in front of the office. After a few moments, he got out, walked over, and pushed open the door. Inside, the warmth hit him. It was like walking into a sauna. Despite being a warm Spring day, the heating in the reception area had turned up. Behind the reception desk, busily tapping away on the keyboard of her computer, sat a blond-haired woman. She looked up as Turner approached, smiled and said, 'Good Morning. Can I help you?'

'I'm looking for Mr Armitage.' He brought out his warrant card and showed it to her. 'I'm Detective Constable Turner. He was out of town on a job when I called on Friday.'

'Yes,' she replied. 'I remember you. It was me you spoke to. If you wait a moment, I'll give Don a call.' She picked the phone up, spoke briefly, replaced it and said. 'If you'd like to follow me, I'll take you to the workshop.' She stood up. She was a small petite woman in her early thirties.

Turner followed her out of the office along a passage to a door marked *Staff Only*. Then, tapping a series of numbers into a keypad, the door clicked open.

'I'm Don's wife, Doreen, by the way. Secretary, general dogs body, and bookkeeper,' she said, pushing open the door. 'Don was pretty intrigued when I told him about the call he got from you on Friday.'

Donald Armitage was sitting at a workbench on the far side of the workshop. With him was another man. Both were staring at a video monitor; then, hearing the door closing, Armitage looked around, got down from his stool and came over.

'Dear, he is from the police. The call I told you about on Friday?' Doreen Armitage said.

Don Armitage walked up to Turner. 'Ah, yes! So, tell what can I do for the police?

'Good morning, sir. DC Turner, Kingsport CID. I hope you can help me with a case I'm working on?'

'Certainly, if I can,' Armitage replied. ' What is it you want?'

'I believe your firm installed the security system at the White Cliffs guest house. Is that correct?'

From back in the reception, the phone started ringing.

'I'll leave you to it, dear,' said Doreen Armitage, addressing her husband. She then turned and hurried away.

Don Armitage watched her go, then said, 'No. Not really. We only maintained it. White Cliffs brought this cheap system from some cowboy installer. It was constantly failing and costing them more callout fees than the system was worth.' He smiled. 'Luckily, she came around to my way of thinking and now has a new, more modern system installed. '

'What happened to the old system? It's the recording unit I'm interested in. There was recently an incident, and I was hoping there was something on it that could help us?'

'It was old, cheap, and useless. Nowhere as good as the modern stuff.'

'Okay. But do you still have it? The recording unit, I mean. Can you still pull stuff from it?' Turner asked hopefully.

'Maybe. Not sure if even if we have it or not!' Armitage turned and addressed the man at the workbench. 'Jim. What happened to the old White Cliffs security system? Did you bin it?'

'No,' he replied. 'Not yet. Haven't had the chance.' He pointed to the window. 'Unless Douglas has tossed it, it should still be in the back of the van.'

Reid sent out a silent prayer.

'Go look, will yer, Jim? See if it's still there!' asked Armitage.

Minutes later, Jim returned carrying a large cardboard box. He set it down on the bench and rummaged through it. Then, pulling out the recording unit, he asked, ' Is this what you're looking for?'

'I'd like to see what's on it!' Turner asked.

'They are not foolproof by any means,' said Armitage. 'One of the few disadvantages of surveillance cameras is that they can be tampered with by individuals. And, because so many cameras watch different locations simultaneously, it is hard for one person to monitor them all. Another disadvantage is that they have blind spots, areas the camera can't turn far enough to see.'

'Yes. I understand all that! Even so. I don't think it applies in this case. But I'd still like to see what's on it,' Turner said.

'Jim, rig it up, will yer please?'

'It'll take him a minute or two to set up. While Jim's doing that, would you like a coffee?'

'Thanks. Milk and two sugars, please.' Turner replied.

While Armitage went off to get the coffee, Turner walked over to the bench and watched as the technician plugged in cables and connected the unit's USB cable to a computer. When finished, Reid asked, 'Can you get specific days on this? Does it have the date and time on it?'

'Well. We'll soon see,' Jim said as he switched on the monitor. The screen flickered, then revealed a still picture. Turner stood looking at the grainy and dark vision from the camera in the entrance hall. The still image was of a woman. The bottom of the screen showed the time and the date.

'That doesn't look good! It's not one of the best systems. This is supposed to be a video, not a blasted still camera,' said Armitage, walking up to the bench. In each hand was a mug of coffee. He handed one to Turner. The still image suddenly disappeared and was replaced by one of the empty entrance hall. Turner saw that the timeline had moved forward by two hours.

Putting the mug down on the bench, Turner asked, 'Is it possible to go too, Thursday, the sixteenth? I'm looking at the timeline between two and three in the afternoon.'

'Well, we can only but try,' said Armitage. 'Give it a go, Jim. See what you can get!'

Turner sipped his coffee and watched as stills and video footage appeared on the screen. Then, after a few anxious minutes, Turner suddenly said, 'Stop. Stop it right there.'

Leaning forward, Turner could see the dark and grainy figure of the woman. He recognised her. It was Marge from the dining room. There was a man, but his back was turned to the camera. Turner watched as the blurry figure moved to the stairs, and then the picture froze.

'Bugger! I'll need a copy of this, please. Now. Can you run it forward? I want to see if that man comes back down the stairs?'

The next recorded image to appear on the screen was one day later.

'Sorry,' said Armitage. 'It's like I said. They were sold a crap system.'

Chapter Twenty-Eight

'That was all that was on it,' Turner said to Reid as he stepped back from the monitor. 'The recording after that was on and off, flashes, bangs and blurs. There was nothing on it we could use. At least we have our visitor on camera.! Too bad they didn't install the new system before the break-in.'

'This has to be the same man responsible for the break-in, and I've got a good idea who that person might be, but proving it is another matter.' Reid said.

Turner gave Reid a quizzical look. 'You know something I don't?' he asked.

Reid thought about the envelope he'd opened in his office earlier, the one Mrs Webster had given him.

'When the time is right, and I've done a bit more digging, you'll know. Until then, I'm saying nothing.'

'Covering your backside?' Turner said, looking at him with a none committal smile.

'If I'm right, we catch our killer. If I'm wrong, I'm out of a job and on the dole.'

'Shit, Mike. Are you serious?'

'Yes, Bill. Deadly serious.'

****

Carter had been lucky and found a parking spot near Mercery Lane. After leaving the car, he walked along towards the Old Butter Market. As usual, the square was crowded with tourists and locals alike. All out for the day, they were making the most of the warm Spring sunshine. Some gazed into shop windows, while others browsed inside, buying souvenirs and postcards. In contrast, others sat at the open-air tables enjoying coffee and snacks.

It had been christened the Butter Market a mere two centuries ago. The name Butter Market was replaced by the not-so-nice name, Bullstake. The name came from when dogs were once used to bait bulls. In days gone by, it was a common belief that it helped make the meat more tender. Carter much preferred the more modern, humane way of tenderising his stake. He placed it on the chopping board and pounded the life out of it with a wooden mallet.

Once clear of the Butter Market, Carter walked along Burgate and eventually turned into Butchers Lane. At the far end of the lane, he could see the cathedral's spire standing proudly against the skyline. Halfway along, he stopped in front of the Dickensian Bookshop and looked in the window. He saw only one person, a man walking slowly along a bookshelf, reading the titles. Customer or owner? Carter thought. The man found what he was looking for and removed it from the shelf.

Before setting out that morning, Carter had looked up Peterson's webpage. The Dickensian Bookshop, it said, set out to be the home of English literature. It boasts books from the Victorian era through to the heyday of the 1920s and the classic period of the 1960s. It also stocked an extensive selection of the best modern authors, focusing on Pulitzer and Booker prize-winners and quality popular literature.

Carter went to the door, pushed it open, and walked it. There was something decidedly Dickensian about the premises. The original floorboards complained beneath Carter's weight as he walked in.

The man turned. 'Anything special you are looking for, sir?' He asked. 'We cater to all readers.'

'Are you Mr Kevin Peterson?' asked Carter.

'Yes, that's me. What can I do for you?' Peterson asked curiously.

Carter came straight to the point. 'I Believe you once knew Adamma Okoro?'

Carter saw the look of surprise on Peterson's face.

'Who are you, and what the hell do you want?'

'Detective Chief Inspector Carter, Kingsport CID.' Carter said, showing Peterson his ID. 'I'm investigating her death. I don't know if you are aware of the fact, but recently, the remains of a female were unearthed at Oxney Woods. They have identified those remains as Adamma Okoro. And I was told you once knew her?'

Peterson froze, stared at Carter, then said, 'Adamma? No. I did not know. You say they found her in Oxney Woods?'

'Yes,' replied Carter. It's been in all the papers and on TV. I'm surprised you never saw it?'

'I've been in Paris all week, Inspector. I was at a book fair and only got back last night!'

'If you don't mind, I have a few questions I'd like you to answer.'

'My God! Murdered! I was told she just up and left, ran away from home. That was what they led me to believe. But even then, I couldn't comprehend why she did it. Neither of us could.'

'Who's us? Carter asked.

'Her friend. All her friends. So! who the hell killed her?'

'That is what we intend to find out. However, I believe the police, at the time, did not formally interview you. Is that correct?'

'Well, yes. All police asked was, where was I at the farm the night she disappeared? I said no, and that was the truth. There was a birthday party over at Broadstairs. A school friend. I stayed the night and came home the next day.'

'How did you get there?' Carter asked.

'Get there? I went to Canterbury and caught the bus. I came back Sunday the same way.'

'Did you give a statement to the officer who spoke to you?'

'Yes. I did. It was an inspector. I can't remember his name, though.'

'Was it Rigby?' Carter asked.

'Yes. Come to think of it, I think it was,' Peterson replied.

Carter knew nothing was on file about a follow-up investigation or even a mention of Broadstairs.

'Did you like her?' asked Carter.

'Yes, I did. I went out with Adamma a few times. I was only eighteen, but my father was a very strict man. He put the mockers on me seeing her. He said she was too young for me and I should stick with good English girls, ones of my age. My father also told me I was to have anything to do with her. He could be violent, so I did as I was told.'

'Did he ever turn violent with you?'

'Sometimes, if he came home pissed, he'd have a go at mum, but she gave as good as she got. She stood up to him.'

'It sounds like he may have been a bit of a bully and prejudiced. Do you think it was Adamma's age he was against? Or was it her colour?'

Without replying, Peterson turned and walked over to the counter.

'Oxney Woods!' said Carter. 'When you were on the parish council, you campaigned to stop the development of a health spa? Why, why was that?'

Peterson turned and faced Carter. He placed the book he was holding down on the counter. 'It's a bit of our history and should be left as it is. The wood was once the site of a Viking settlement. If you don't believe me, talk to the museum's curator, Rob Boyd. He was the one who first discovered it. They even have relics from the site on display there.'

'And that is your only reason for preserving it?' asked Carter.

'What are you referring to, Chief Inspector?' There was anger in his voice. 'I hope you don't think I had anything to do with her death. Because if you are, you're barking up the wrong tree. I would never have harmed her.'

'I was not referring to anything like that at all.' Carter paused, then said. 'What can you tell me about Liam Crawley?'

'Crawley! Now there's a name from the past. A square peg in a round hole, if ever there was. Creepy, as we used to call him. He never fitted in.' Peterson stared at Carter. 'You don't think he had anything to do with it.do you? Have you spoken to him?'

'No. We haven't, not as yet. Just one last question before we go? Do you believe your father was capable of murder?'

'A bully, yes, he was. A drunk, yes, he was. But a killer, no. He was too much of a coward,'
Carter saw the unmistakable look of hatred in Peterson's eyes. Carter nodded. 'Okay. Thanks for your time, Mr Peterson. Please call me if there's anything else you may remember, no matter how small. It might help catch Adamma's killer,'
Carter placed his calling card on the counter, thanked Peterson, walked to the door, opened it, and left. He stood on the pavement, thinking. Then, after a few minutes, he turned and headed to his car.

Chapter Twenty-Nine
Tuesday

Reid found the cottage, standing, as George Archer had said, right next to the church. The cottage was in the old-fashioned black-timbered style, with one larger and one smaller pointed gable. He pulled the car into the curb and got out. Looking over the low hedge, Reid saw an elderly woman sitting under a trellised porch knitting. Next to her sat a man reading a newspaper. None noticed as he pushed open the gate and walked down the path toward them.

'Mrs Chester?'

They both looked up in surprise.

'My, my. Where did you spring from?' asked the old lady. 'Yes. I'm Mrs Chester. Who's asking?'

A wizened face peered out from around behind the newspaper. 'Who are you?' the old man asked. He took off his glasses and focused his eyes on the new arrival.

'A friend of yours, George Archer, suggested I call on you. He said you might help me?' Reid said.

'George sent you, did he?' she asked, nodding her head slowly.

'Yes, he did. I'm Inspector Mike Reid from Kingsport.'

Mrs Chester and her husband exchanged glances and then looked at Reid. 'Help you with what?' Mrs Chester asked, laying down her knitting.

'It's about your days at Ripton Hall,' replied Reid. Mr Archer said you worked there for many years. 'I'd like to ask you a few questions?'

'Yes. That was sixty-five years ago. I was fifteen when I first started in the kitchen. I ended up becoming the housekeeper,' she said.

'Ripton Hall. Well, well, well. I think we'd best go inside and make a pot of tea, don't you?' the old man said to his wife.

'Yes, Walter. I think we should!' Then, from where she was sitting, she looked over at Reid.

'Oh, I'm Gwen, and this old sod, here, and by the way, is Walter.'

'Nice to meet you both,' Reid said.

The old man stood and walked off into the cottage. 'Hey! Less of the old. I'll 'ave you know, woman, some down the pub still fancies me!'

She gave a hag-like cackle. 'In your dreams, you old bugger. You talking about old Mary?' She's been blind for years. She gave another cackle. 'C'mon, inspector. Let's go inside, shall we?'

They followed the old man in.

'Please. Take a seat,' the old man said

Sitting down at the kitchen table, Reid asked Gwen Chester, 'Do you know this girl?' He produced the two photographs from his pocket, which he'd found in Wilson's room. He laid them out in front of her.

She picked up a pair of glasses that were lying on the table. After putting them on, she studied both pictures for a moment, frowned, and then said, 'Yes. It's the young housemaid from over at Ripton Hall, Maria Jankowski. This one was taken on the steps at the back of the house, and this one,' she said, tapping it with her bony finger, 'was taken on the lawn outside the Summer house. I recognise the flower bed. That takes me back a few years.'

Reid slowly stirred his tea, the spoon clinking on the sides of the cup. 'What can you tell me about her?' he asked. Gwen Chester sat conjuring up the past for a moment or two, then said, 'A sad story.'

'Why?' asked Reid. 'What happened to her?'

'She got too close to the master, or should I say, he got too close to her! The servants back in that era were enslaved people by another name. Nothing was their own, not even their own bodies, especially the young girls. They both tried to keep it secret, but we all guessed what was happening.' She looked across the table at her husband. 'You remember her, don't you, Walt?'

'Aye,' replied the old man. 'I do. A pretty young thing. Used to come into the village sometimes to do a bit of shopping. Maria was always smiling.' He laughed. 'Now we know why.' He laughed again.

'Behave, you silly old bugger,' she said. She turned back to Reid. 'Anyway, Maria was there six months before her ladyship found out. She was dismissed and sent packing. We found out later it wasn't the first time for his lordship. He'd been carrying on with one of the village girls. I know it wasn't the same after Maria left. His lordship withdrew into himself. He was quiet and often moody. I think he had genuine feelings for Maria.' She paused and said, 'If you don't mind me asking. Why all the questions? Has she done something wrong? Is she in some kind of trouble?' Gwen Chester asked.

'No. I'm sorry to say Maria died some years ago. Her name came up in a case we're investigating, and we wanted some background information. We're looking into the death of her son, Maurice Wilson.'

'Marie Wilson? So, she got married, did she? Had a boy called Maurice?'

Reid decided not to tell her the whole story. 'Yes,' he said.

'Ah, now come to think of it,' Walter Chester said. 'I think I saw something about him in the local newspaper. Found dead in the graveyard, wasn't he?'

Reid nodded. 'Yes, at Corn Hill. Thank you,' he said. 'You've been most helpful, and thanks for the tea. Most refreshing. I'll leave you to get on with your day.' He then stood and buttoned up his jacket.

'Oh. Off now, are you? I was about to bring out the scones and jam. Made them fresh this morning. Still warm, they are! Sure, you won't stay and have one?'

'That's very kind of you, Mrs Chester, but much as I'd like to, I'd best be getting back.'

'Well. I'll tell you what, inspector. How about I give you some to take back, and then you can have them later? Sound good?'

He smiled and nodded.

****

'Okay. This is just a catch-up session. I want everyone to be on the same page,' Carter said. He looked around at everybody. 'I've spoken with Kevin Peterson this morning, and I'm convinced he had nothing to do with Adamma's death. So, we can safely cross him off the list. However, I had thoughts about his father, Martin Peterson. So, I asked Kevin whether he thought his father was capable of murder. Still, according to Kevin, his father was a bully and a drunk but not capable of murder, so we can also cross him off our list. Not that it helps, even if he was capable of it. He's dead. Died five years ago.'

'So now that just leaves Liam Crawley?' said Marcia Kirby.'

'Yes, Marcia. We'll get to him later.'

Hollingsworth turned to Bill Turner. 'The security footage from the guest house. Did the lab have any luck making the image any clearer?'.

'No. Luke,' said Turner. 'It's too blurred to make out. It's a man, though.'

The swing doors at the end of the room burst open, and Mike Reid walked in. He walked across the room to where they were gathered around Jill Richardson's desk. He placed the cake tin down.

'Where the hell have you been all morning?' Carter asked him. 'I tried to call you.'

Reid took out his mobile. 'Bugger! Sorry. Flat battery.' He looked back at Carter. 'I've been chasing up a hunch. I went to see the housekeeper that once worked at Ripton Hall, Mrs Chester. After talking to her, I see a much clearer picture. I have a good idea why Wilson was murdered and who killed him?'

'What's in the tin?' asked Hollingsworth.

'Scones. Half a dozen. Jam and cream.'

'Whoa! lovely. Who are these for?'

'For anyone who wants one! All courtesy of Mrs Chester. Tuck in, help yourself.'

Hollingsworth didn't need telling twice. He opened the cake tin, took his time selecting one, and then handed the container to Dave Lynch, saying, 'If anyone doesn't want theirs, I'll have it.'

'Tell us something we don't know, Luke,' said Lynch sarcastically.

Hollingsworth replied, raising the middle finger of his right hand.

'Well, talking of Wilson! I've just found something,' said Jill Richardson, looking up from her computer screen. 'This explains why Wilson was in the graveyard and what he was searching for. I went through the parish records. It said that Maria Jankowski was buried at St Augustine's. According to the plot numbers and where Wilson was found, it was Maria Jankowski's headstone he was leaning against!'

'Now it's all making sense,' said Mike Reid, looking at those around him. 'Bare with me. Let me get my head around this. I need a few moments to think.'

They focused all eyes on Reid. Then, a few moments later, he said, 'This is what I think happened.'

Before Reid could continue, Dave Lynch's mobile buzzed. He held up his hand as a sign of apology and then walked away to answer it. He spent a while in muffled conversation with the caller, then returned.

'That was Micheal, John Stukey's younger brother from the wine shop! When I was there, I asked John if he'd sold any Johnnie Walker Blue Label locally. He said no. Now it turns out that Lord Peter came in and took a single bottle. He took it from his monthly order and was served by Micheal Stukey. Stukey said he's forgotten to mention it to his brother. Lord Peter didn't explain why he wanted it. Stukey thought that strange but didn't question it. I asked when that was, and it turns out it was the same day Maurice Wilson died! There was one other thing he told me. Lord Maurice is dead. He died in his sleep last night.'

'So, Lord Peter has now inherited the whole of the Ripton empire?' said Marcia Kirby.

'Yes, he has. All four hundred and six million quid's worth of it,' said Jane Little. 'El Supremo. Numero Uno.'

'Seems you've been doing your homework, PC Little,' Carter told her.

'I can't take all the credit for it, sir,' she said. 'Google has to take some of it!'

Chapter Thirty

'Yes. That puts an entirely new slant on things.' Reid said. He looked at Carter. 'I want all of Peter Ripton's movement checked for the night of Wilson's death.'

'You still think it's him?' Carter asked.

'Yes, I do,' answered Reid.

'You were about to tell us why you think Ripton is responsible?' said Dave Lynch.

Reid looked straight at him. 'It all comes down to money, Dave! I think he planned to meet Wilson at the graveyard that night. And furthermore. I know why he murdered him.'

'This all sounds far-fetched,' said Kirby. 'Why would a man with all his money want to kill?'

' That's it. The money! He wants to hang on to it. It's the same reason he killed Andrew, his brother. Peter was the oldest and next in line to inherit. But, remember. Peter was out of the loop, not to be trusted with money. So, Lord Maurice gave control of it to Andrew.'

'How the hell are you going to prove he killed his brother?' asked Carter.

'I can't. The only way to do that is for him to confess.' Reid said.

'What else do you have?' asked Dave Lynch.

'I'm guessing that Wilson worked it all out, then went to Ripton Hall to confront Lord Maurice. I also think he told Lord Peter Ripton why he wanted to talk to him.'

'Worked what out? Told Peter Ripton what?' Carter asked.

'That Maurice Wilson was Lord Maurice's bastard son,' Reid said. Reid then told them about what he had learnt from Gwen Chester, Ripton Hall's ex-housekeeper.

Reid stopped to let them absorb what he had said, gave it a few moments, and then continued speaking. 'Lord Maurice is down on the birth certificate as the father of Maria Jankowski's baby,' Reid said. 'Wilson sent for a copy. We have it. It arrived at White Cliffs the other day. Mrs Webster gave it to me yesterday when she came in. I'm sure Lord Peter broke into his room at White Cliffs. I think he was looking for the same thing.'

'Being older than Peter, Wilson could claim his rightful place in the family, next in line, and in my book, that's a bloody good reason for Peter to murder him. Don't you think?' Turner said, looking at those around him.

'Lord Peter Ripton must have Wilson's laptop and phone. I want the tape from his security camera on his gate for the night of the break-in. I'm sure it will show him leaving.'

'You think a magistrate or even a judge will grant a warrant. Do you think he'd let you walk in and grab that from a peer of the realm, purely on your belief?' said Jill Richardson.

'Yes. I think we have enough evidence to support it,' said Reid.

'But he was in London on the night of the murder?' said Hollingsworth. 'They picked his Ferrari up on two ANPR cameras heading up the M2! at three o'clock that afternoon.'

'Yes. That's what is bothering me. But Ripton could have easily slipped back, met up with Wilson, given him the doctored whiskey and then gone back to London. There is also the fact that the Ripton estate once used 1080 for fox control. I know because George Chester told me it's still stored in the shed, and they also use rabbits laced with strychnine.' He stopped for a moment or two, then said. 'Has anyone checked out to see if they picked up his car on the return journey?' He looked at them. His question went unanswered. 'No? Right! Luke. I want you to get on to it. I want it checked.' Hollingsworth nodded. 'That could take a while. I'll get on to it..'

'There is one person who would know if he left home on the night of the White Cliffs break-in,' said Marcia Kirby, staring at Reid.

'Who's that?' Reid replied.

'The nurse,' Kirby said. 'Rita Mercer. Now that the old man has died, she'd be out of a job. I doubt Ripton will keep her on now. She could be your answer. There's no point talking to the housekeeper, Mrs Dutton, as she lives out and comes in daily.'

'Yer, you're right, Marcia. Find out whether Mercer's moved on yet. She may even be registered with an agency.'

****

Hollingsworth stood inside the CCTV monitoring room at the traffic control centre and stared up at the bank of monitors.

'Here it is,' said the operator, leaning back in his chair. He pointed to the screen on his desk. 'That's the one you're after, the Ferrari?'

Hollingsworth turned his attention away from the monitors. Instead, he looked at the one on the desk the traffic controller was pointing at.

'Yer. That's the one,' Hollingsworth said, looking at it.

'It was picked up crossing Vauxhall Bridge at eight twenty and then again on the A2, the M2 and A299.' He clicked the mouse button several times, letting Hollingsworth see the still images of Ripton's Ferrari taken by the ANPR cameras.

'Is that helpful?' the man asked.

'Yes and no,' Hollingsworth replied. 'Thanks. Can I have the stills of these?'

'Yep. Could you give it a couple of minutes? I'll be right back.'

Will the man was away, Hollingsworth jotted down the recorded time the Ferrari was seen. When the man returned with the prints, Hollingworth thanked him, then left.

Ten minutes later, he was back in CID. He went straight to Reid's office and stood in the doorway.

'Seems you were wrong about Ripton. Sorry! There's no way he could have been in that churchyard the night Wilson died.' He walked in. 'I've checked with ANPR. We've got him on camera driving up Friday afternoon and driving back Saturday morning. He never came back that night. He left London just after eight. Last seen heading home outside Whitstable at nine-thirty-five.' He handed over the pictures.

Reid looked at them, then stood up and walked to the window. Staring out over the rooftops, he said, 'Something's not right here. I can feel it. He's as guilty as sin, and I will prove it.' As he said that, the mobile on his desk buzzed. He went and picked it up. On the screen, he saw it was an unknown caller.

'DI Reid.'

'Mr Reid. You said to call if I remembered something.'

'Who's this?'

'It's me, Marge. Marge from the White Cliffs guest house. Do you remember? I told you about the man that came here looking for Mr Wilson.'

Reid tapped the speaker icon, allowing Hollingsworth to listen.

'Yes, of course. Mrs Tucker. You've remembered something, have you?'

'No, not really.'

'Oh! Okay then, what was it you wanted?'

'That man. The one who came looking for Mr Wilson. I've just seen him again.'

'Where. When was this?'

'Today. Just now. Right here.'

'You mean he's returned?'

'No. That same man in the newspaper. The Gazette. There's a picture of him with a group of people. He's one of them. It's him, for sure. It's on page seven. He's in the background. He's the third one from the right.'

'Does it name him?'

'No, it doesn't. It only gives the names of the two people that have just got some business award.'.

Hollingsworth turned and walked over to where Marcia Kirby sat at her desk. He said something to her and started rummaging and emptying her waste bin. Then, finally, Hollingsworth found what he wanted and waved it above his head. Reid saw he had a copy of the Gazette. Reid remembered seeing it on Kirby's desk earlier in the day.

'Mrs Tucker, can you just hang on for a sec while I check it out?'

Hollingsworth came back, sorting through the pages and put it on Reid's desk. Both stared down at the picture.

'Are you sure this is the man that came to visit Mr Wilson, Mrs Tucker? The third one on the right.'

'Yes, I'd swear to it. Yes, it's that man. It's definitely him.'

'Okay, that's good. I'd like you to pop into the station and make a formal statement. Can you do that for me?'

'Yes, I can come in tomorrow if that's ok?'

'Until tomorrow, then? And thanks for your help.' He said goodbye, hung up, and then, picking up a texter, drew a circle around the head.

Kirby came and stood in the doorway. 'What's going on?' she asked. She walked further into the room.

'Our mystery man. The one who called on Wilson at White Cliffs. We now know who he is. We have his picture.' Reid told her of the phone call he'd just received and pointed to the newspaper on his desk. Kirby bent her head and stared down at the picture. Then, she lifted his eyes, and with an expression of perplexity, she turned to Reid like she was seeking an explanation and said, 'But that's Lord Peter Ripton. So. He was he who visited Wilson?'

There was a smug expression on Reid's face. 'Yes, Marcia, it's him, and tomorrow we'll find out why.'

Chapter Thirty-One

Wednesday

As Reid and Kirby made their way up the steps to the front door of Ripton Hall, it was already open and standing there, waiting to greet them, was the nurse from their first visit, Rita Mercer. She no longer wore her green scrubs but was now dressed in jeans and a white blouse, her hair tied back in a ponytail. When Reid buzzed the house from the main gate, a woman's voice answered. It must have been her, Rita Mercer. Reid was surprised to see her still in place. He thought she would have left.

He introduced himself. 'We're here to see Lord Peter.' Reid said as he approached her.

'He's out somewhere with his visitor at the moment, inspector. I'm not sure if he's on the estate or not. If you'd like to come in and wait in the morning room, I'll see if I can find out where he is.' She took led Reid and Kirby across the large open reception area. Opening the double doors, she showed them in.

'Please make yourselves comfortable, inspector. I'll go call him. I'll be back in a moment.' She walked off, quietly shutting the doors behind her.

'He won't be too pleased to see us,' Kirby said, looking around the oak-paneled room. One wall had shelves crammed full of books. And on the others, hung paintings. All the furnishings, she noticed, were very similar to those in the summerhouse where they had first spoken to Ripton. However, the fabric on the chairs and settees was blue silk, not red. There were French windows that opened out onto an entertainment area. Outside was a slatted roof pergola from which hung wisteria. There was a table, comfortable armchairs and a refreshments trolley. An ice bucket was set out on it and ready for use. In it was a bottle of champagne. Two glasses sat empty. Maybe this was his guest, she thought.

The door behind them opened, and Rita, the nurse, returned. 'He's off the estate, I'm afraid. He'll be back in about an hour, maybe two, and then he said he'll come to Kingsport to see you. I might add that he sounded angry.'

Yer, I bet he did, though Reid

'When he returns, can I tell him what you wanted?'

'No, thank you. Just tell your husband if you wouldn't mind. Can you ask him to pop into the Kingsport police station? I'll be happy to see him there.'

Kirby stepped forward. 'I was sorry to hear about his lordship,' she said. 'It must have come as a shock, especially after having nursed him all that time?'

'He was not a healthy man. It's a miracle he lasted as long as he did. Mercifully, he passed away peacefully in his sleep. He was eighty-five,' Rita Mercer said.

'So! I take it you'll now be looking for a new position?'

'I've already been offered one.'

'That's nice. Where are you off to?' Kirby inquired.

'Nowhere. I'm right staying here. Lord Peter has asked me to stay on the job of running the house for him. He intends to have more staff and get a permanent chef. It will take some of the pressure off of Mrs Dutton. She is getting on a bit and ready to retire. Well, if you'll excuse me, I have work to do. If you'd like to follow me, I'll show you out.'

Reid decided not to quiz her about Ripton leaving the estate on the night of the break-in.

As Mercer closed the front door on them, Reid's cell phone beeped twice. He looked at the display. It was Jill Richardson. He walked down the steps to the car and lent against it, listening to what Richardson had to say.

After a few minutes, he slipped the phone back into his pocket, opened the car door and got in. He looked at Kirby as she sat there struggling with her seat belt.

'That was Jill. Turns out she's had an interesting chat with the night porter at the Parkside Hotel. Turns out, he's a relative of Jane Little, and he had something very interesting to tell her about Lord Peter.' As they drove back, he told Kirby what Richardson had said.

****

Luke Hollingsworth slowed the car and turned off Ramsgate Road. A few minutes later, he and Carter were heading along Victoria Parade. To the left was Victoria Park, the bandstand, and behind that, the clock tower. Beyond it, the sea and Viking Bay. Passing the bandstand, the hands on the clock tower showed nine-fifteen.

'I thought Roger Earnshaw said Crawley had a funeral parlour in Manston, not Broadstairs?' said Carter, staring out the side window.

'If I remember rightly, what Earnshaw did say was, it was somewhere around Manston,' replied Hollingsworth. 'That covers quite a sizeable area!'

'Take the next left,' said Carter, looking at the screen on his mobile. Hollingsworth followed Carter's instructions.

'It should be about halfway along here.' Then, a few seconds later, 'Ah, there it is, over there on the right,' said Carter.

A sign said there was parking at the rear. Hollingsworth turned down the side street and drove through the open gates into a courtyard. Over on one side was a three-bay garage. Inside sat three cars, a hearse and two Bentley limousines. Leaving the car, they walked back out along the street and around to the front of the funeral home.

'I wonder if the term coffin originated from cough-in?' Hollingsworth casually asked as he stood looking at one in the display window.

Carter gave him one of his questionable looks.'

Hollingsworth saw it and, justifying his statement, said, 'In the old days, the plagues and influenzas killed so many that a cough often signified the end? I wonder, too, if "fin", being the French word for "finish," is part of the word?'

Hollingsworth pushed open the door and walked in. Before Carter had time to close it, a woman appeared from behind a black velvet curtain. Carter put her in her late forties. She was dressed in a dark business suit, her dark hair cut short, like a young boy's.

She smiled. 'Gentlemen, how may I be of help? Are you here about a departed loved one?'

'No. I'm Detective Chief Inspector Carter, and this is Detective Constable Hollingsworth.' Carter said, showing her his ID. 'We are from Kingsport CID. We want to speak to Mr Liam Crawley, please. Is he about?'

'No. I'm afraid not. My husband is at our Dover branch and won't return until later. Is there anything I can help you with? I'm his wife, Gemma. May I ask what it's about?' she inquired.

'It's something that happened a long time ago. I hope Mr Crawley can help us clear up a few things.'

'I hope that it's not something not too serious?'

'It concerns the death of a young girl in 1991. We're trying to locate and interview everyone who knew Adamma back then. Your husband was one of them.'

Gemma Crawley looked at Hollingsworth, then back to Carter. 'That was thirty-odd years ago. My God. Liam would have only been, what, a teenager back then? Do you honestly think he'd still remember after all this time? And you say that Liam knew her?'

'Yes, he did. Liam and some of his friends knew her. He and Adamma both lived in the same village. Did he ever tell you that?' Carter replied.

'Adamma. Unusual name?' she said. 'No, he never did.'

'Adamma Okoro.' Hollingsworth said. As an afterthought, he added, 'She was a Nigerian.'

Gemma Crawley looked at her watch.

What Carter saw set his heart racing. 'That bracelet. Where did you get it?'

'Yes, quite eye-catching. Many people have commented on it over the years. I love it because Liam gave it to me on our wedding day, July 1997. He had it engraved.'

'Can you give me his phone number, Mrs Crawley? Maybe I'll give call him myself?' He waited for Hollingsworth to jot down the number Gemma Crawley gave him. He then thanked her, turned and walked towards the door.

As they headed down the street to the parking area, Hollingsworth broke the silence by saying, 'I didn't take you for jewellery sort of person.'

'Normally, no. But in this case, Luke, yes. So I thought you, being the apparent smart arse you think you are, would have spotted it?'

'Spotted what?' Hollingsworth asked indignantly.

'Spotted that Gemma Crawley was wearing Adamma Okoro's missing bracelet. The one with the gold pendant. The one shaped like the map of Nigeria. It was what Adamma was wearing the night she disappeared. There's no way there'd be another one like it. So, it has to be hers!'

'Shit. No. Bloody hell. I didn't see that. Aren't you going back and talking to her?'

'No, Luke. I saw it all on her face. There's no way Gemma Crawley knew where that came from or who it belonged to. It's Liam we need to talk to. I think he's our man?'

As they were about to get into the car, Hollingsworth leaned across the roof and said, 'So, now what, boss? Do we go to Dover and pull him in?'

'No, not at the moment. When we get back, I want you to get that group photo of Adamma, the one where Crawley has his hand on her shoulder. I want that part of it enlarged.' Hollingsworth looked across at Carter and said, 'Why?'

'At the moment, Luke, it's a long shot. But if I'm right…' Hollingsworth waited for Carter to finish the sentence. It went unsaid. Instead, pulled out his mobile.

'You drive. I will call Crawley and get him and the wife to come to Kent Street. If I'm not mistaken, Gemma Crawley is already on the phone with him, asking who Adamma was, and if I'm right, you can bet your boots, he's, at this moment, shitting bricks.'

Chapter Thirty-Two

After Reid had given Jill Richardson instructions for the search warrant, she left, closing the door quietly behind her. Reid then got up from his desk and strode purposely out and across the room to where Marcia Kirby sat, gazing intently at her computer screen. Her head was moving from side to side as she read the night porter's statement. Reid was about to say something when the phone on her desk rang. She grabbed it, listened, nodded her head a few times, said thanks and placed it back on the receiver. Kirby looked up at Reid.

'That was the front desk. His lordship has arrived. They've stuck him in interview room two. He's come armed with his lawyer.'

Reid looked up at the clock. 'Okay, Marcia. You ready for this?'

'Yer. Let's see him wriggle his way out of this one?'

****

'So, Inspector. What is it this time, inspector? Did I not make myself clear the last time we met?'

Reid pulled the chair out from under the table and sat down. He looked across at the man sitting next to Ripton.

'This is Mr Mortimer Banyon, of Banyon and Croft, inspector. He is my legal representative. He was visiting me at the estate today, which I was told, you already know because you have already been there? So, I brought him with me, thinking he might come in handy if I have to sue the police for harassment.'

The words were not lost on Reid. To Reid, Ripton was as arrogant as ever. He still thinks he has the backing of a higher god, Chief Constable Tom Bishop, thought Reid. But, don't worry, my old son, Reid thought. When Bishop discoverers what you've been up to, he'll drop you like a hot potato.

Mortimer Banyon's voice, when it came, was one of high breeding.

'Good morning Inspector. His lordship has already briefed me on your last visit.' Then, looking at Kirby, he asked,' And I take it you, young lady, must be Detective Sergeant Kirby?'

'That is correct.' She then added. 'This interview will be recorded.' She sat down and switched on the machine. She gave the time and date and asked those around the table to identify themselves.

Mortimer Banyon was a dapper thirty-year-old dressed in a light grey, pin-strip suit. He wore a white shirt with a grey, matching pin-stripe tie. With his thin moustache, slicked-back hair and wide smile, he reminded Reid very much of the manager of a five-star hotel he once stayed at while on his honeymoon.

'In answer to your question, Lord Peter, we have some additional evidence regarding the death of Maurice Wilson. We need to ask you some further questions. Also, a search warrant has been issued for Ripton Hall and is underway as we speak.'

Ripton's face turned pale. 'What are you looking for?' Ripton asked. He turned and faced Banyon.

'Yes! What are you looking for?' the lawyer asked.

'We have grounds to believe that Lord Peter Ripton was involved in the death of Maurice Wilson.'

'What evidence do you have? Just what is going on here?' Mortimer Banyon asked. 'This is a serious accusation.'

'This is a ridiculous accusation.' He banged his hand down hard on the table. 'I had nothing to do with that man's death,' Ripton shouted.

Kirby opened the file and slid it across to Reid. Reid ran his eyes over the page, refreshing his memory.

'The dead man, Mr Maurice Wilson. You said you only contacted him once, and that was when he came to see you on your estate. Is that correct?' asked Reid.

'Yes, that's right. For God's sake. The man was a menace?'

'I have it on good authority that you saw him a few days later. We have a witness on the staff who states you visited Wilson at White Cliffs on Thursday afternoon, the sixteenth of March, two days before he died.' Reid stared across the table, saying, 'I'd advise you to consider before answering.'
'Well, whoever it was, was mistaken,' replied Ripton.

'I am quite prepared to bring that witness in and put you in a line-up. Would you prefer that?'
Banyon lent over and whispered something into Riptons ear. Ripton looked crestfallen, then said, 'Okay, I admit it. Yes, I went and saw him. All I wanted to know was what he wanted to say to my father.'

'And did he tell you that?' Reid asked.
Ripton's mouth moved, but no words came out.

'You don't have to answer that,' Banyon said.
Kirby asked, 'Lord Peter. On Friday, the seventeenth, I believe you attended a meeting in London and stayed overnight at the Parkside Hotel. You didn't return to your estate until the following morning, Saturday the eighteenth. Is that correct?'

'Yes,' came the reply. He looked at Mortimer Banyon. 'For God's sake, man, say something. It's what I pay you for,' Ripton growled.

'Hear them out. Let's see what they have to say first. Then, if I say otherwise, you answer, no comment.'

'You returned that same night. After you drove to London that afternoon, you hired a car? The desk clerk at the hotel confirmed he made a booking in your name! Why did you need a hire car?' asked Reid.
Ripton looked at Banyon and then back to Reid. Ripton answered. 'Mine was acting up, so I wanted to get it looked at.'

'Where did you send it to?'

'A garage in Knightsbridge. I can't remember the name of it,' Ripton replied. 'I'd been drinking.'

'You just said you never left London, then why was it that the same car you hired was seen travelling south on the motorway at 9.30 pm? Traffic cameras picked that car on the A2 outside of Canterbury and again at the Duke Of York's roundabout, and then at St Margaret's-at- Cliffe 90 mins later. Traffic cameras picked up that car later, just after midnight, travelling the same route back to London.'

Ripton looked uneasy. Reid's statement was met with an awkward silence.

After a few moments, Banyon asked. 'Do you have proof Lord Peter was the driver?'

Kirby said, 'According to the CCTV cameras, Lord Ripton's returned the car to Reece Hire at 2.34 am. It shows Lord Ripton as being the driver. ' Kirby handed Banyon a still picture taken from Reece's Hire Car CCTV. It was of Ripton getting out of the car. 'We also have his signature on the hire documents.'

Banyon gave Ripton a concerned look.

Reid took over. 'I know that after Maurice Wilson came to see your father, you went to the guest house where he was staying. At some point, I think he told you that your father, Lord Maurice Ripton, was also Wilson's biological father, and he would prove it. We now know this to be true because he sent off for a copy of his birth certificate.' Kirby removed the copy from the file and passed it across to Ripton. 'A baby named Maurice Jankowski was born to Maria Jankowski in December 1988 at Saint Paul's Convent. He was brought up and educated by the nuns until he was adopted and took and then took the name of Wilson. As you can clearly see. The father named on the birth certificate is Maurice Ripton. So, if I'm not mistaken, unless your father's last will and testament state otherwise, that would make Maurice Wilson your half-brother. Being older than you, he had a legal right to the family fortune. A half-brother rates equally with the full brother, which meant that each of you would be entitled to half of the estate.'

Kirby said, 'I think he told you he'd sent off for the certificate, and after his death, you broke into his room hoping to find and destroy it.'

'What break-in was this?' asked Banyon.

'All in good time, Mr Banyon,' said Reid.

As Ripton read it, his face turned pale. He passed it to Banyon.

'I'm sure a simple DNA test will disprove all this nonsense,' Banyon said confidently.

'I'll tell you what I think,' said Kirby, leaning forward and staring into Ripton's face. 'I think he told you about your father's affair with his mother, Maria. She was seventeen at the time and worked at Ripton Manor as a maid.' Kirby gave him a knowing look. 'Wilson told you where he was staying, then after you saw him at the guest house, you set up a meeting with him in the Corn Hill churchyard. We have checked your phone records. You called, and you set up the meeting for that night. Before that, you had already set about planning his death. Being older than you, Wilson would be first in line to inherit a fortune. It was something you had no intention of letting him have. You wanted it all to yourself. So, being the greedy man you are, you devised this plan to give yourself an alibi by pretending to be in London during that time. After driving from London that night, you met him in the churchyard, and it was there that you gave him a bottle of whiskey, the same bottle you picked up from Stukey's the wine merchant that very morning.' She placed both hands down on the table. 'Yes, we know all about that. You then laced it with a lethal cocktail of 1080 and strychnine. He was drunk when he arrived at the estate. You thought he would be an easy target? All you had to do was lace his drink.'

'You can't prove any of this,' Ripton said.

'Let's stop it right there, shall we, inspector? I think it's time I had a word alone with my client,' Banyon said.

Chapter Thirty-Three

Hollingsworth pulled open the door leading into reception, then stood back and allowed Carter to enter. A man who appeared to be drunk was leaning against the counter, arguing with a constable. The drunk paused as Carter approached him and scowled. He was unshaven and clearly unwashed, his fly was undone, and all his shirt buttons had been done up in the wrong holes. Without hesitating, Carter walked straight passed the man and over to where Liam and Gemma Crawley were seated, leaving Hollingsworth standing guard by the door.

'Thank you both for coming in this afternoon.'
Liam Crawley's eyes darted first to Hollingsworth and then back to Carter. 'What is it you want, chief inspector? Gemma said it had something to do with that girl, Adamma Okoro? For your information, inspector, I hardly knew her.'

'I think you can help us. In fact, I'm sure of it.'

'Why am I here?' asked his wife. Concern showed on her face. 'Why do you want me?'

'Mr Crawley. Liam. If I may call you that?' said Carter, trying to put Crawley at ease. 'If you wouldn't mind going with Detective Constable Hollingsworth, I'd like a word with your wife. I'll be along shortly. I'm sure he can get you some tea or coffee while you wait.'

Looking unsure, Crawley hesitated for a moment, then said, 'I have a business to run, so I can't stay too long.' Carter smiled and nodded.

Reluctantly, Liam Crawley followed Hollingsworth through the door. Once he'd left and the closed, Carter said. 'If you'd like to come with me, I'll explain exactly why I've asked you here.'

****

Holding the bracelet up to the light, Carter said,' So, now you understand why we need to speak to your husband. We want to know precisely how Liam came to have it in his possession.' Carter rose from his seat. 'I'll need to keep this.'

Gemma Crawley looked up at Carter. 'Can I see him, please?'

'At the moment, I'm afraid that's not possible. However, if you wish to stay, I'll have someone bring in some refreshments.'

'I'm sure this is a big mistake and can easily be cleared up. I'm convinced that Liam knows nothing about that girl's death.'

****

As Carter walked along the passage to the interview room, Reid and Kirby came out of interview room two. They stood to one side, allowing Ripton and Banyon to exit as they were escorted off along the corridor by a constable.

'Have you charged him?' Carter asked Reid after they'd passed.

'Not at the moment, no. Ripton has turned up armed with his lawyer. I'm waiting to see what the search team comes up with.' Reid stared at the departing trio as they made their way down the passage. 'I'm sure he knew what we wanted, which was why he brought his lawyer with him.'

'Right,' said Carter, 'I'll leave you to it. Crawley has come in. Good luck with Ripton.' Carter turned away and walked off.

Reid and Kirby set off along the passage, and as they got to the door at the end, Bill Turner came through.

'I've left the team back at the estate and came straight back with these. They found these in Ripton's desk.' In his hand, Turner held three evidence bags. He held up one that contained a red Samsung tablet, then held up the second. In it was a mobile phone.

'Are they Wilson's?'

Turner nodded. 'Yes. No doubt about it. I checked them out.'

'Two nails in his coffin.' Reid smiled at Kirby, saying, 'There is a god, after all.'

'We've got his lordship by his royal balls,' she said.

'Well done, Bill. Did they find the 1080 and the strychnine?'

'Yes, they have. It was on a shelf, not locked away. Anyone could have gotten to it. I've sent them off for fingerprinting.'

'What's in the other bag?' asked Kirby.

'Diaries. I had a quick look. The name Maria crops up quite a lot of times. Surely, that has to be Maria Jankowski. In one, he even writes how he missed her after she went. That's not all we found either because I checked out his security video, and It shows him leaving the night of the break-in. I think it's worth investigating further. Maybe I'd visit the traffic control centre and check the traffic cameras?'

'Ok,' said Reid. 'C'mon. Let's look at what we got on this tablet.'

****

Kirby and Watkins sat in the observation looking out through the one-way mirror at Ripton and his lawyer.

'He certainly doesn't look comfortable. But, on the other hand, maybe he knows what's coming.' said Commander Watkins. She looked up as Mike Reid came into the observation room. 'Are you sure you got this inspector?' said Watkins to Reid. Are you comfortable with this, inspector? I hope you've dotted the I's and crossed the T's?'

'Yes, ma'am, I am. We've got everything we need.' He looked at Kirby as if seeking confirmation. She tapped the files she was holding.

'Okay,' Watkins said. 'This is a high-profile case. He's a peer of the realm. The press will soon be all over this. So you stuff this up, and you know where you'll end up, don't you?' She left the rest unsaid.

Without saying a word, Reid then turned and left the room. Kirby followed him out. Watkins sat down and waited.

Seconds later, Reid and Kirby walked into the interview room. Kirby closed the door, went over, and sat beside Reid. The room was sparsely furnished. It held just the bare essentials: a table, four chairs, two on either side. The chair in which Ripton sat creaked as he moved about. Reid picked up on the body language. Clearly, Ripton was uneasy.

The fluorescent lighting gave everything in the room a slight bluish-green cast. On one wall, facing Ripton, the two-way mirror. Behind this, Reid knew Watkins was watching his every move, listening to his every word. Four wide-angle cameras, positioned in each corner, covered the room.

Kirby leaned across and set the recorder running. 'Interview recommenced at,' she looked up at the wall clock, 'Three ten pm.'

Reid saw by his face that Ripton was not the defiant and cocky man he looked before. Instead, he suddenly looked exhausted, drawn and haggard.

Reid opened the file that lay in front of him. He looked up.'I have a letter sent to the convent one week before Maria Jankowski gave birth. It's from a law firm in London. In fact, Mr Banyon, it's your firm, Banyon and Croft.'

Banyon looked up in surprise, his eyebrows flicking upwards.

Reid continued. 'It says here that while the baby is in the care of the nuns and until it is adopted, the convent will receive the sum of two hundred pounds a month.'

'May I see it please, inspector?'

Reid handed the letter across to him. Banyon read it, then turned to Ripton, saying, 'This is 1988, two years before you were born. I don't recognise the signature because it was well before my time. This was back in my father's day. I'll have to check into it.'

'I strongly believe those instructions came from your father,' Reid said, Looking at Ripton.

Kirby quickly directed a question to Ripton. 'Am I correct in saying that you knew nothing of this?' she asked? I would strongly advise you to think about that before answering?' Banyon nodded at Ripton as if giving him permission to talk. This session, though Kirby, was to be lawyer-approved answers only.

'Yes, you are. How on earth would I know about it? I did not have any knowledge of this. None. I am saying no more.' Ripton replied.

'Then can you tell me why, when conducting our search, officers found Wilson's tablet and phone locked away in your desk? They also found some of your father's old diaries. We have been reading them. It tells the complete story. It reads like a romantic novel, which I'm sure you were fully aware of. You must have read it; otherwise, they wouldn't have been there in the first place, would they?' She waited for his reply. None came.

Reid said, 'So, It's clear that you knew everything about what happened between your father and Maria Jankowski. When Wilson claimed to be your stepbrother, you saw an immediate threat to your empire, and from that moment on, he had to go. Am I correct?'

'This is ridiculous. It's a farce. So, I'm saying no more,' said Ripton.

'One other thing.' Kirby looked directly into Ripton's eyes. 'The matter of the break-in at White Cliffs! Your CCTV has you leaving your estate just after midnight. Traffic cameras picked up your Land Rover in several places, and one of them a little later picked you up going through Saint Margarets Bay.'

Ripton sat saying nothing.

Reid took over. 'We have enough evidence now to formally charge you. Lord Peter Ripton. I am charging you with the murder of Maurice Wilson. You do not have to say anything. But, it may harm your defence if you do not mention when questioned something which you later rely on in court. Anything you say may be given in evidence. Do you have anything to say?'

Ripton looked crestfallen and looked at the lawyer. Banyon slowly shook his head.

'No'. Ripton replied.

'Don't worry, Peter. I shall apply for bail. I'll have you out by the morning.' Banyon.

'This interview is now over,' said Reid, giving the time. Kirby leant across and switched off the recorder.

Chapter Thirty-Four

When Carter walked into the interview room, Luke Hollingsworth was leaning back in his chair, arms folded, silently staring at a very nervous-looking Liam Crawley.

'Sorry to keep you waiting, Liam. ' Carter closed the door behind him and said. 'Can I get you some tea? Coffee?'

'No, thank you. Your man here already asked,' he said, nodding his head at Hollingsworth. 'I want to know why I have been dragged down here? I was in the middle of organising a funeral. What's this all about? You mentioned Adamma Okoro. What about her? Your colleague here won't tell me.'

Carter came over to the table, pulled a chair out from under it, and sat down next to Hollingsworth.

'I must caution you that you do not have to say anything. But, it may harm your defence if you do not mention when questioned something which you later rely on in court. Anything you do say may be given in evidence. This interview will be recorded. You are entitled to legal representation. Do you wish to have a lawyer present?'

'No, I don't want one. Why would I want a lawyer? I've done nothing wrong,' said Crawley indignantly.

'Because we are conducting a murder investigation. By law, we are required to inform you of your rights. So. If you don't want a lawyer, then I'm sure you wouldn't mind answering a few simple questions?'

'I know nothing about any murder. Who is dead?'

Carter guest Crawley already knew the answer to that. 'I understand you knew Adamma Okoro? Did you know she was dead?'

Carter saw the body language. Crawley's hand came up to his mouth. Carter had seen it many times during interviews. It wasn't an act of surprise. Instead, it showed that the next thing Crawley was about to say was false. 'No. I didn't.' He paused quickly and then said, 'Well, yes. I did. Come to think about it, I think I saw something about it in the newspaper.'

'Did you ever go out with Adamma?'

'No, never.'

Carter looked down at the open file in front of him. 'According to her parents and some of her friends that we've interviewed. They said you had. You even met her parents.' Crawley took a few seconds to answer. 'Well, um, yes. I did go out with her once or twice. It was such a long time ago. I just forgot about it.'

'You seem to have forgotten quite a few things?' Carter said. He picked up the evidence bag and took the bracelet out. 'Liam. Have you ever seen this before?' he asked.

'Yes. It belongs to my wife. What are you doing with it?'

'Well, at least you remember that. Can you tell me how you came to be in your wife's possession?' Carter asked. Carter saw the sweat forming on Crawley's brow.

'I gave it to her on our wedding day. Why do you ask?'

'I'll explain, but first, I want you to tell me where you got it from?'

Crawley hesitated for a moment before saying, 'Erm… An antique shop in Canterbury.'

'Which one?' Carter asked.

'It was so long ago, I can't remember.'

Carter fixed his eyes directly into Crawley's. 'And I suppose you're going to tell me next. You no longer have the receipt?' To break from the stare, Crawley shifted his gaze over to Hollingsworth.

'Of course, I don't. My God, man, that was years ago. How long must I stay here? I've answered all your questions, and I have work to do, and now I must go.'

'If you help up by answering all of our questions, maybe you can go back home with your wife. Otherwise, we can hold you for questioning for a further twenty-four-hour. It's all up to you, Mr Crawley,' said Hollingsworth.

Knowing what he'd done would be etched on Crawley's mind forever, Carter asked. 'Where were you the night Adamma went missing?'

'I can't remember. It was such a long time ago.'

Carter looked at the bracelet. 'I know all about his. Shall I tell you a little about its history?'

Crawley tried to look disinterested. 'If you must.'

'For your information, it's one of a pair, and that gold charm on this one is a map of Nigeria. What I'm holding here is the one that once belonged to Adamma. They were a matching pair. Both of which she was wearing the night she disappeared. Did you know that even after all this time, DNA can still be present, so when we send this off to the lab to be tested, I bet you we'll find not only you and your wife but also that of Adamma's as well?'

'In fact, Mr Crawley, we have that twin right here,' said Hollingsworth taking it from the evidence bag and holding it up for him to see.

'I've changed my mind. I'm saying no more until I've spoken to a lawyer.' Carter turned off the recording, rose, went to the door and said to the constable standing outside, 'Take Mr Crawley to the custody suite and let him phone his lawyer. Then he can be taken along to the lawyer's briefing room. He can cool his heels in there until he comes.'

Walking down the corridor some minutes later, Hollingsworth turned to Carter and laughed. 'I'm surprised that bluff of yours worked. Was that wise boss telling him there was still DNA on it? That was a bit of a gamble. If he believed that, then he'd believe anything. I hope his lawyer doesn't get to hear about it. If he does, we could lose him through entrapment.'

'Don't worry about it, Luke, he won't. Crawley is more gullible than I thought he was. It's all a show. I took him to be an intelligent man, but he's not. I've seen his type before.

Crowley's not that smart. He's trying to bluff his way out of it.' Carter thought about the ring. 'Anyway, I still have one more ace up my sleeve to play yet. Get me some coffee and a couple of those jam doughnuts from the canteen, will you? It'll be some time before the duty solicitor turns up. In the meantime, I'll tell his wife she can go home.'

Chapter Thirty-Five

Luke Hollingsworth stuck his head around the side of the door. 'Boss. Crawley's lawyer's here. He's down in reception.

'Okay, Luke. Put them together and when they're done, let me know. We've already had one excellent result today. Let's see if we can make it a double.' Carter looked up at the clock. 'With any luck, we can have this all wrapped up by teatime.'

'Mike and Marcia really went all out with that one. I honestly thought Ripton would get away with it. He just caved in. The Chief Constable won't like him much now. I bet his face will be red when the press finds out that his lordship was a buddy of his. They were quick off the mark and had already been on to Commander Watkins. She's set up a press conference for five, so when that gets aired on the six o'clock news, it will show the aristocracy isn't above the law? Hollingsworth said.' He shook his head, laughed and said, 'There you go! He's fallen from grace. From rich man to poor man in one fell swoop.' He then turned and walked out.

Remembering the lecture, Watkins had given to him and the others about keeping clear of Ripton, Cater thought, I bet he's not the only one that will be backtracking. As Hollingsworth walked across the room, he again thought she was only passing on the Chief Constable's words. She really has nothing to reproach herself about. He sat there for a while wondering why, after all this time, the pair had kept up their affair. After all, he was a married man. Maybe she's good in bed? His thoughts were interrupted by a cough. Looking up, he saw Mike Reid standing in the doorway.

'You'd better come and hear what Bill Turner has to say. When his lordship hears about this, it will piss him off big time.' Reid's face broke out with a wide grin. 'I can't wait to see his face when I tell him.'

Gathered in a group a few minutes later, Turner told Carter and the others about the phone call he'd received from Sister Agnes at the Saint Paul's Convent.

'Well,' Turner said. 'Turns out Sister Agnes'. He looked at the questioning face of Hollingworth. 'She's the librarian and archivist at the convent. She said she found some documents that had been misfiled. Among them were some of Maria Jankowski's. It turns out that she had twins and was born twenty minutes after Maurice. I've asked her to send copies of them here to me.'

'That's a bit of a turn-up for the books? But the letter from Banyon and Croft only mentions one child?' said Kirby, looking over at Reid.

He looked back at her. 'There's also nothing in the old man's diary about twins, that's for sure,' replied Reid. 'Maybe he just didn't know?'

'I can see now, Mike, why you can't wait to tell him,' said Carter. 'Somewhere out there is another heir to the Riptons millions.'

'Canada,' said Turner. 'He's in Canada. That's where he was taken to three days after he was born. It's what Sister Agnes told me was in the document!'

'Does this twin have a name?' asked Carter.

'No. But there is a name of the adoptive parents,' replied Turner.

' I guess, then, that he'll have to be traced. When you get that information, Bill, pass it on to Ripton's lawyers, will you? They need to go look for him. That's their job, not ours.'

At that moment, the phone in his office started ringing. He turned and walked off to answer it. He returned a few minutes later and said to Hollingsworth, 'Crawley's lawyer is ready.' He rubbed at his eyes. 'Come on, Luke, let's get this over and done with. Let's do this. I want this finished.' Thinking Carter was looking tired, Hollingworth followed him across the room and through the door.

Chapter Thirty-Six

The solicitor, who introduced herself as Ms Jane James, who was now sitting on the other side of the table, was not what Carter had expected. She was a petite woman. Although he knew most solicitors, he had not seen this woman before. But, short as he was, this woman looked like she had a colourful upbringing; her pantsuit was grey over a red blouse, and her hair was mauve with green streaks. Her skin was dark. Carter guessed she was Jamaican. In contrast, behind black-rimmed glasses, she had very prominent blue eyes. Carter wondered if she also wore colourful underwear?

Jane James spoke. 'I would like it to go on record Detective Chief Inspector that my client came here of his own free will to help and is willing to assist you in any way he can.'

'Duly noted,' said Carter. He looked at Crawley and then said, 'And please remember you are still under caution. Do you remember this?' he asked Crawley. 'For the tape, I am now showing Mr Crawley exhibit 4A, a photo.' Carter passed it over. 'Is that you with your arm around Adamma's shoulder?'

He gave Carter a strange look. 'Yes, it is.'

'And the ring on your finger, do you recognise that?'

'Yes. Obviously.' Another strange look. 'What is this? What's it all about?'

'You'll find out in a moment. Where is that ring now?' Carter asked.

'I don't know, that was years ago. I think I lost it! Yes. Come to think of it, I did,'

'Well, I have news for you.' Carter removed it from the small evidence bag and sat it on the table. 'We found it.' Crawley was clearly shocked. He picked it up and examined it.

'Is this your ring,' Hollingsworth asked.

'Yes. Where did you find it?' Crawley asked.

'It's where you dropped it when you buried Adamma. We found it, along with her remains. You killed her, didn't you?

Jane James leaned over and whispered in his ear. Crawley looked at her in surprise. He stared at the solicitor as if unsure. She nodded. 'If it's true what you told me before, then yes, it's for the best.'

Crawley rubbed the palms of his hands together. Fear and uncertainty showed on his face. Carter knew that the next words to come from his mouth could land him in prison for a very long time. He again looked at the lawyer, who again nodded. 'Tell them what you told me.'

The words came out in a sob.'It was an accident. Honest, it was. I didn't mean to do it, I swear.'

'Chief Inspector Carter. The charge against Mr Crawley is involuntary manslaughter, a common law offence. It's not premeditated,' said James 'It was an unintended death resulting from an assault.'

'Okay. So tell me, Mr Crawley, what exactly did happen? Please, take your time.'

He took a few deep breaths to compose himself, then said. 'After picking strawberries that afternoon, I went home and had tea and then later, I went back to one of the huts. Some of the strawberry pickers, returning to London the next morning, were having a bit of a party. When I left there to go home, I bumped into Adamma a few hundred yards up the road. She told me she'd been to Canterbury to see a show. She climbed over the style and took the path, a shortcut across the field through the woods to go home. I stood there and watched her go.'

'Then what happened,' Carter asked.

Crawley took a deep breath, then said. 'I thought about it for a while. I wanted to ask her out, but she'd reached the edge of the woods by then, so I ran to catch up with her.' He brought his hands to his face and covered his eyes like he was trying to clear the vision.

'What happened when you caught up with her. Where you drunk?' asked Hollingsworth.

'No, I don't know, I can't remember. May I have some water, please,' Crawley asked.

Carter nodded at Hollingsworth, who rose from his seat and left the room. He returned in less than a minute, poured the water into a plastic beaker and handed it to Crawley, who gulped down the water and placed it on the table. He took his hanky out of his jacket pocket and wiped his lips.

'Please continue when you're ready,' Carter said to him.

'When I caught up with her, I asked, would she like to go to the pictures with me on Sunday? She said no. I asked again why but she just got furious. She told me to stop pestering her and leave her alone, that she was going out with Kevin, and that she didn't like me or want to go out with me. Adamma called me creepy. It wasn't very respectful then she walked off. I yelled at her that she was a bitch. She turned, threw her bracelet at me, and told me to go and leave her alone. She then came back and slapped my face. I just pushed her. That's all I did. She fell and hit her head on a rock.'

'What did you do then,' Carter asked.

'She wasn't moving, not breathing. I panicked and ran. I knew she was dead, so I returned to the farm, got a shovel and buried her. I didn't mean to kill her, honest I didn't. It was an accident."

****

Sitting in the Black Bear an hour later, Hollingsworth finished the pack of onion-flavoured crisps he'd been eating and said, 'That came out of the blue! Great result. You played the ace card you had up your sleeve and won. That photo, boss, really sealed his fate. I see now why you asked me to get it enlarged.' Hollingsworth raised his glass. 'Here's to you, boss, and your determination. Cheers.' They all joined in the toast.

Carter looked around the table, thinking that now it was over, it was the right time to bring it up. Go out on a high, he thought. Carter had already told Watkins on Friday. Now it was just a matter of telling those sitting around him. He pictured the house in Spain.

'Thanks, all of you. I want to say how proud I am to be working with you all. It was a team effort. You all deserve the credit. Well done, take a bow, put your party dresses on and have some fun. But right now there is one important announcement I would like to make......

Printed in Great Britain
by Amazon

48378857R00106